SO-BRA-344

"You won't stab me in the back during this…caper?"

"I wouldn't call it a caper. Although, it will require a bit of…finesse."

"Meaning?"

This was the part she wouldn't like. The part that would have been easy with another woman. But Julia wasn't easy. She didn't respond to Ferro's flirtation. Didn't respond to his charm. Charm he knew was lethal in most cases.

"We'll have to make our merging look organic."

"And how do you propose we do that?"

She wasn't going to like his suggestion, but that, in some ways, made it even more perfect. The more flustered she was, the more control he would have. "It would be completely expected for a couple to discuss a project and come to the conclusion that collaboration would be the best for all involved."

Her blue eyes glittered. "Are you suggesting that we…that we feign some kind of personal involvement?"

"You're sanitizing it," he said, smiling. "I'm suggesting we pretend we're heavily involved in a scorching affair."

All about the author…
Maisey Yates

MAISEY YATES knew she wanted to be a writer even before she knew what it was she wanted to write.

At her first job she was fortunate enough to meet her very own tall, dark and handsome hero, who happened to be her boss, and promptly married him and started a family. It wasn't until she was pregnant with her second child that she found her very first Harlequin Presents® book in a local thrift store—by the time she'd reached the happily ever after, she had fallen in love. She devoured as many as she could get her hands on after that, and she knew that these were the books she wanted to write.

She started submitting, and nearly two years later, while pregnant with her third child, she received The Call from her editor—at the age of twenty-three she had sold her first manuscript to the Harlequin Presents® line, and she was very glad that the good news didn't send her into labor!

She still can't quite believe she's blessed enough to see her name on not just any book, but on her favorite books.

Maisey lives with her supportive, handsome, wonderful, diaper-changing husband and three small children, across the street from her parents and the home she grew up in, in the wilds of southern Oregon. She enjoys the contrast of living in a place where you might wake up to find a bear on your back porch, then walk into your home office to write stories that take place in exotic, urban locales.

Other titles by Maisey Yates available in ebook:

Harlequin Presents®

Maisey Yates

THE COUPLE WHO FOOLED THE WORLD

HARLEQUIN PRESENTS®

If you purchased this book without a cover you should be aware
that this book is stolen property. It was reported as "unsold and
destroyed" to the publisher, and neither the author nor the
publisher has received any payment for this "stripped book."

Recycling programs
for this product may
not exist in your area.

ISBN-13: 978-0-373-13163-1

THE COUPLE WHO FOOLED THE WORLD

Copyright © 2013 by Maisey Yates

All rights reserved. Except for use in any review, the reproduction or
utilization of this work in whole or in part in any form by any electronic,
mechanical or other means, now known or hereafter invented, including
xerography, photocopying and recording, or in any information storage
or retrieval system, is forbidden without the written permission of the
publisher, Harlequin Enterprises Limited, 225 Duncan Mill Road,
Don Mills, Ontario M3B 3K9, Canada.

This is a work of fiction. Names, characters, places and incidents are
either the product of the author's imagination or are used fictitiously,
and any resemblance to actual persons, living or dead, business
establishments, events or locales is entirely coincidental.

This edition published by arrangement with Harlequin Books S.A.

For questions and comments about the quality of this book,
please contact us at CustomerService@Harlequin.com.

® and TM are trademarks of Harlequin Enterprises Limited or its
corporate affiliates. Trademarks indicated with ® are registered in the
United States Patent and Trademark Office, the Canadian Trade Marks
Office and in other countries.

Printed in U.S.A.

www.Harlequin.com

THE COUPLE WHO
FOOLED THE WORLD

To my friends who waited in movie lines with me for hours…dressed as elves. You made being a geek fun. And to Pippa, for getting all my jokes. This hero is for you.

CHAPTER ONE

"IN TERMS OF design and usability, the new operating system is leagues above the competition." Julia Anderson turned and gestured to the high definition monitor behind her, the one that was currently projecting the interface of her computer screen to thousands in the audience, and millions watching on television and the internet worldwide. "It's sleek, user friendly and aesthetically pleasing which, as we know, matters. Technology is not just about wires, it's about people."

She smiled for the cameras, knowing she looked good. Thank God she had a personal stylist, along with a hair and makeup team these days. On her own she was hopeless. She'd been told so many, many times. But with a legion of people making sure she looked presentable, she could face the world—and it was literally the world—with confidence.

"However, design isn't everything." She took another breath and looked down at her computer. "It has to be secure. The new firewall we have in place is more secure than anything else on the market. It's able to identify and block even the most sophisticated threats so that your most sensitive data is protected."

The screen in front of her flickered and a video popped up in the center, then enlarged to take up the entire monitor. She froze, all eyes on her, and on the gigantic display behind her that was showing the exact same thing she was currently looking down at.

"Secure? I don't find it all that secure, Ms. Anderson. Maybe secure against the rare hacker who bothers to use Anfalas. Anyone running Datasphere software would be able to get right in."

Heat prickled on her neck. Her face. Ferro Calvaresi was a pain in her butt that would not quit. Though, in fairness, she was also a pain in his. And they were a mutual pain in Scott Hamlin's. Basically they were a circle of techie annoyances to each other, but this, this was going way too far.

His face, his gorgeous, infuriating, chiseled face, had effectively taken over her presentation, his smug smile a gigantic display of a weakness in her firewalls she hadn't known about.

"Hardly just *anyone* running Datasphere, Mr. Calvaresi," she said, trying to keep calm, aware that her humiliation was being broadcast everywhere. The launch of her new OS was the news of the day. The launch of every Anfalas product was the news of the day. And Ferro had just hijacked it. "You practically need a masters in technology to run Datasphere. On the other hand, Anfalas computers focus on the user."

"And your user just got hacked. I wonder if you have any banking information on here I might access?"

She made an axing motion toward the guy running the feed between her computer and the screen and the screen behind her went dark, at the same time the audio for Ferro was cut. His voice was still coming out of her laptop, and his face was still visible to her.

"And you're done here," she said, glaring daggers at the computer screen.

She looked back up. "I apologize for the theatrics. You know how my competition can be. It's entirely possible he's trying to compensate for some shortcomings." There was a wave of nervous laughter through the room.

The press were jostling in the front row, but they knew better than to start flinging questions at her before the designated time. She was strict about that. She liked to make her presentations uninterrupted.

Grrrrr.

A new computer was supplied for her and she continued on with her demonstration. Of course, the wind had been taken out of the sails of the security portion of her speech, so she opted to skip on to the ultra high definition features of her new monitors, and to demonstrate the music and photo editing software, the things that hit really bit with her target market.

And when she was done, she opted to dodge the press. She dashed off the stage, cursing and taking a water bottle from the cooler in the back, then jammed her sunglasses onto her face and took her black leather bag from her assistant.

"Car?" she asked.

"Out back. Press is being baited by a fake car out front." Thad picked something off the shoulder of her black T-shirt. "Stray hair," he said.

"Thanks." For everything. She wanted to cling to her assistant and cry right then, but Thad would scold her for smudging her makeup, and she shouldn't show that kind of weakness anyway. Because the weak were unceremoniously devoured, in life and in business, and she didn't show vulnerability anymore for that very reason. She knew that all too well.

What she would do was go home to her mansion on the seaside, look out the window at the view and eat a gallon of ice cream. Oh, yes, calories, here she came. And then... oh and then she was going to plot her revenge against Ferro Freaking Calvaresi.

She pushed open the back door and got into the limo that was waiting, closing the door tightly behind her.

"Hi."

Her head whipped to the side and her jaw went slack. There was Ferro and his mocking smile, in the very male flesh.

"What the—? What are you doing in my car?"

"It's my car. These limos all look alike."

"Well, what did you do with *my* car?"

"I sent your driver on. Told him you had a ride. And a meeting. With me."

"Was that a meeting for me to punch you in the face for that stunt you just pulled?"

"Are we suddenly forgetting about what happened at my last product launch?"

Julia bit the inside of her cheek. "What?"

"All of the swag bags at the product reveal for Datasphere's new smartphone had your OnePhone in it. And then you had that slogan projected on the wall…"

"OnePhone to rule them all." She laughed. "It never gets old."

"It's old."

"Disagree. But anyway, the fact is, your presentation wasn't nearly as high profile as mine. A bunch of tech heads getting their specs fix. My presentations are events."

"Only because you make a spectacle about every product you unveil."

"It's my signature, okay? People like it. It caters to my clientele. I'm a trend, Calvaresi. You should try it sometime."

"A trend, huh? Why don't you ask acid-washed jeans how that worked out?"

"I'm an evolving trend," she bit out. "My products stay relevant." She leaned back in the seat and the car started moving. "Where are we going?"

"My office."

"I'm done working for the day," she said.

"No, Julia, you aren't. Not unless you want to miss out on the chance of a lifetime."

"I just had the chance of a lifetime in there." She looked down at her manicure. Her hands didn't even look like hers anymore. No more chips and glitter. Her rough edges were being polished away nicely. Well, the rough edges of her looks. The social thing was a bit harder. She could cover the geek girl up with paint and cool clothes, but she was still there. She could just never show that poor, weak vulnerable girl to the world. Never again. "I get chances of a lifetime all the time." She looked back up at him. "Chances most people never get. Why? Because I work hard. Because I'm a genius, yes. But the hard work, too. That means, if I pass up *this* chance of a lifetime, another one will happen before dinner."

"I wouldn't bet on it."

"You seem so sure."

Ferro leveled his dark gaze at her, a smile curving his lips. "You've been contacted by Barrows."

"How did you know that?"

His smile widened. "I wasn't sure until just now. But so have I. And so has Hamlin. We've all been tapped to design the new navigation system for their fleet of luxury cars."

"Have we?" she asked, keeping her voice monotone. This offer had been about the biggest thing to hit since her One-Phone had become the bestselling mobile device in the United States. A chance to have her devices in cars all over the world? A huge deal. Massive. And she was apparently dealing with stiff competition if she hoped to get it.

"We have. And if you want it, I can help you get it."

"I don't need your help."

His expression didn't falter. "You do. I've made you look incredibly vulnerable. A bit inexperienced and unprepared, even. You may need my help more than you realize."

She gritted her teeth. It was the v word she hated most. "Catch."

"What?"

"Catch, Calvaresi, what's the catch?"

"You'll be seeing a lot more of me," he said, winning smile firmly in place. Ugh. He was so annoying. And hot. Which was even more annoying.

"Why? Because if you intend to pull more stuff like this, you can bet I won't be happy about seeing more of you."

"Most women are very happy to see more of me."

"Most women don't rival you for net worth and the position as head of the most profitable tech company in the world. Boom. Headshot."

"Most women are also not such a spectacular pain in my ass. But I'm willing to let it go for the greater good."

"Greater good?"

"I'll be straight with you. I can't land this account. Neither can you. I lack the...simplicity that your technology has."

"You aren't user friendly."

"I haven't dumbed anything down to create mass appeal unless necessary."

"Snob."

"Anyway," he continued. "I lack the tech necessary to make the navigational devices simple and smooth for the average driver. You lack the sheer power I possess. You know my processors are superior to yours and they last longer. Hamlin, well, he can provide a mediocre version of my processor and your interface. Not as good on either end, but his processor is better than yours and his interface is better than mine."

"And you know this how?"

"Corporate espionage, how else?"

"That's not right."

"As if you've never done it to me."

She feigned a sneeze and looked out the window at the California scenery scrolling by. Rolling hills dotted with stucco walled-houses with red roofs and the jewel bright sea beyond. Even after seven years of living on the coast, the view took her breath away. It had been her new start to her brand-new life. A true reboot.

Thankfully it never got old since she needed a nice breathtaking view to distract her from Ferro and all of his questions and smiles and that spicy, masculine way he smelled.

Which was hard to ignore in the enclosed space of the limo. A lot of tech guys had a smell a bit like they'd been living in a cave. And some of them even had a permanent hunch from bending over the keyboard. Had she not hired an image consultant, she very well might have ended up that way herself. Because frankly, in her life, she'd become much more concerned with coding than how she looked to the world. When she'd tried on her own, she'd always come out looking ridiculous. Without a consultant, she was hopeless.

But Ferro wasn't like that. He exuded a kind of easy charm and sex appeal that most people with his level of intelligence, including her, rarely bothered with.

Not that she could achieve sex appeal, even with professional help, even if she did bother, but it was a nice thought.

"I'll take your silence as affirmation and move on," he said, his tone dry. "I don't want Hamlin to get the account, mainly because *I* want it. I'm sure you feel the same way about both of us."

"Yes," she said, still scanning the shoreline, keeping herself distracted. The limo wound up the side of a hill and she whipped around to look at Ferro. "I thought we were going to your office?"

"My home office."

She frowned. "Why?"

"I'm not advertising any kind of alliance with you until I've had time to figure out how I want it to look."

"For a man proposing a partnership of some kind you used the word *I* a lot."

"Problem?" he asked, one dark eyebrow arched.

"There's no *I* in team, Ferro, which you may have heard."

"I hate clichés."

"They're cliché for a reason. Because they're true."

"Not necessarily," he said.

The limo pulled around a corner and up to a security box with a facade in the same white stucco that was on the houses. It was shrouded by palm fronds and large, flowering plants so that it almost faded into the lush background.

Ferro leaned out the window of the limo and placed his thumb on a scanner. His driver did the same. "You, too," he said.

"It won't recognize me."

"I know," he said, "and you won't be given clearance to use your print to open the gate. But I keep records."

"Fingerprint records! Talk about paranoid."

"Don't I need to be?" he asked.

She shrugged and nodded in grudging agreement. Especially since she was one reason he should be paranoid. She wasn't above snooping for secrets. But he did it to her, too, dammit. Fair was fair. Or two unfairs made it fair...or something.

"Now, you. Print," he said.

She looked across the seat, across him and out the window. "You want me to just...lean over and do it?"

A flicker of amusement sparked in his eyes. "Yeah. Just lean over and do it."

Her cheeks heated and she did her best not to make eye contact or show him that he'd disturbed her in any way. She was used to men. She worked with a lot of men, and she'd gotten to the point where their innuendos didn't really bother her. Especially not when she had her armor on. The face she showed the world. The leather clad, boot-wearing, tough chick who took no prisoners in the boardroom.

That's just who she would be now. Who she would remember she was now. He was trying to unnerve her. And she didn't back down. Ever. Not for any man.

She took a breath and leaned over, reaching past him. And came up short of the reader. She cleared her throat and edged a little closer, her arm skimming his chest. Her heart tripped and fell, sending a pang of something deeply disturbing through her body. Something that left her feeling a little breathless and shaky.

And there was the way he smelled again. Closer, she could identify the nuances to it. Spice from aftershave. Soap over skin. Clean, musky, masculine skin…

At least, that was her assumption of what the smell was. She wasn't overly familiar with the scent of men's skin, but that was not anything she should be thinking about. And she way shouldn't be thinking about the way Ferro Calvaresi's skin smelled.

Scan your thumb and run, you're regressing!

Regressing to that sad, longing teenage girl she'd once been. Failing to fit in until she'd stopped trying. And then her parents had started trying for her and things had gotten really bad. And then she'd found out what could happen when you tried. When you were vulnerable and soft and trusting.

She shook off the memory, leaned in a bit more and tried to ignore it when the edge of her breast touched his biceps. She tried, also, to ignore the fact that her breath was jammed in her throat and she couldn't inhale or exhale anymore.

She extended her hand and placed her thumb over the scanner, the trapped breath exiting in a gust when it beeped and she could get herself back over to her side of the limo, with a bit of healthy distance between Ferro and herself.

They continued up the driveway and another gate barred

the way. The limo stopped and her heart fluttered against her breastbone like a caged bird. "Are you kidding me?"

He shrugged. "This one just uses a code."

He keyed it in on the screen of his phone, a phone that she noticed wasn't as sleek or fast as the one her company had just released, and the gate opened.

"Neat," she said.

"Does your phone link up to home security?"

"No. But it has really cool gaming apps."

"How is it that your phones are outselling mine?" he asked, dark brows locked together.

"Did you not just hear me say the words *really cool* and *games*? That's how."

"There is no practical use in that."

"Right, and practicality is fine, but the vast majority of people do not have security that screams 'I'm paranoid.'"

"And how is your security?" he asked.

"It screams 'I'm paranoid.' But I don't need to control it from my phone."

He lifted his phone. "Admit it, though, it's very…cool."

"All right, fine. It is."

"This is all making my case very nicely for me." The limo pulled up in front of a massive home, more reminiscent of an Italian palazzo than of the other homes that were set into the hill side.

"What case is that?"

Ferro opened his door and got out, then rounded to her side, opening the passenger door for her. He leaned in and she caught the scent of him again. Her heart tripped over itself again. And then he offered her his hand.

"Stuff it, Calvaresi, this is a business meeting." She got out of the car, avoiding his touch, and leaned past him, closing the door herself. "If you wouldn't do that for a male business rival, don't do it for me."

"I shall make a note of the fact that my touch disturbs you."

"Disturbs me? Your touch *nothings* me. But I won't have you engaging in subtle power plays here. Tell me what it is you want so I can get back in the limo and make my way back down Fort Ferro and back into civilization. I'm in serious need of some wine at this point in the day."

"Then come in and have some," he said. "Because this isn't going to be a brief meeting."

"Oh, no, it is, because I can already tell I'm not going to like what you have to say."

"You won't like it, but you aren't stupid. That means you'll listen."

"Does it?"

"Yes. My case is this. You have something I need, I have something you need. The only way we're going to get this deal is by joining forces."

"I would rather be thrown into the fires of Mount Doom."

"Noble. But it isn't going to get you your deal. Working with me will."

"Wrong. It will get me half a deal."

"It's better than no deal. And it's better than Hamlin getting the deal."

"And why am I more okay with you getting the deal than Hamlin?" she asked. She knew Scott Hamlin was a big-time jerk, she wasn't unobservant and the word about him that she heard was never good. She'd hired people who'd come from Hamlin Tech for low level positions and their view of their ex-boss was never flattering. But then, she imagined people who were let go at Anfalas had bad things to say about her and her executives.

She'd scalped a few of Ferro's employees, too, and the word *tyrant* came up once or twice. And, if she was asked to sum up Ferro Calvaresi, *nice guy* wouldn't be her words of choice.

But, neither of them had ever been accused of sexually

harassing employees or female tech bloggers, either. Hamlin was a chauvinist pig with a capital *oink,* in addition to being generally unscrupulous. And if there was one thing she could not stand it was jackass men who thought they were entitled to a woman's body just because they were men, or because they paid her wages, or whatever lame excuse they came up with to justify their behavior.

So, yeah, for that? She wanted Hamlin to fry. But she wasn't going to come off as too eager to Ferro, either.

"The fact that you have to ask proves that you aren't very familiar with Hamlin."

"I'm pretty familiar with you and I'm not especially fond of you." She looked down at her watch. An extravagant, custom-made piece with her patented OnePhone interface built into it, and started the stopwatch. "You have one minute to convince me to go in, Calvaresi, or I walk."

"Sorry, *cara mia,* I don't work that way."

"So you aren't even going to try?"

"I only have one thing to say on the subject. Better the devil you know than the devil you don't."

CHAPTER TWO

"Is that supposed to intrigue me?"

Annoyance coursed through Ferro's veins and the blame rested squarely with Julia Anderson. But then, it often did. The woman was a menace.

And she was continuing the trend. No one spoke to him like this. No one treated him like this. But then, very few people were so close to being equal with him. Julia's company had come up from nowhere five years ago and had fast gained worldwide popularity. Anfalas was dedicated to bringing the technology fantasies were made out of into reality.

Needless to say, her vision was a popular one. Creative vision combined with an aptitude for all things tech that came naturally to her in a way he hadn't witnessed with anyone but...well, anyone but himself. It made her quite formidable.

Though she fancied herself more formidable than she was. She'd proven that without a doubt today. Acting as though she could turn his offer around on him? Assume the power in the situation?

Not likely.

"It was," he said. "And it did."

"Did it?" She crossed her arms beneath small, perfectly formed breasts and tilted her head to the side, blond hair cascading over her shoulder in a wave. She was dressed in all black, her signature look. Ridiculous when they lived on the

California coast, but he imagined she thought it made her look like a badass.

In his estimation, it made her seem like a pale, spindly, wannabe-goth chick, but she hadn't asked his opinion.

"There has to be a reason you're breathing so hard," he said. "It's either interest in the project or in…me." He flashed her his best smile, the one he knew for a fact made women melt in their overpriced shoes. He had the attraction game down to a fine art. He was an expert in enticement. Ironically the women he'd always worked to entice hadn't truly needed it, but they liked to play like they did. Liked to be seduced. It made them feel desired, and when a man could make a woman feel desired…he ended up with all the power and no need to strong-arm.

"Well, it's not interest in you, so we can check that off the list," she said, her lips tight.

He'd honestly thought as much. Julia seemed to have a serious aversion to him. But he could use that against her just as effectively as he could use a feigned seduction. There was always an in with people. Always a vulnerability. A weakness.

Except with him. Not anymore. Eventually a weakness was hit at too many times and it healed over with scar tissue far too thick to penetrate again. Ironic, how a weakness could develop into the hardest point to breach. But it had happened in his life.

"So it must be interest in my plan. In which case, I would ask you to come inside where we might speak privately."

"You have security that rivals the Pentagon, I'm pretty sure we're private anywhere on your property."

"I never take chances."

"Is paranoia a cultural thing?"

"What?"

"Are all Italians similarly paranoid?"

"Perhaps if they grew up on the streets of Rome. That has

a tendency to make you a little paranoid." A little paranoid. A little lawless. It had a way of searing the conscience so that all the bad decisions just rolled off like water.

Well, not quite all of them. But that was all right, too. Because some lessons needed to be remembered.

"All right. Well. I can see how that might make you a bit more…cautious. More so than me because…the suburbs of Ohio aren't exactly mean."

"Now that we've gotten the basic information easily found in our bios out in the open, would you like to come in and hear what I have to say?"

She squinted, blue eyes glittering from behind a thick fringe of lashes. "Not especially. But I will."

"So, I do intrigue you."

"Don't let it go to your head."

"This way." He put his hand on her lower back and he felt her tense beneath his touch. She was certainly jumpy around him. No melting. No lingering looks. The woman didn't respond in the way other women did. It would make her more difficult to manipulate. More difficult, but not impossible.

"Would you do that to a male colleague?" she asked once they were through the double doors of his home and in the spacious antechamber.

"Can't say that I would. But you are not a man, so stop asking me to treat you like one."

"I want to be treated like an equal."

"Was that somehow not treating you like an equal?"

"I…well…you were treating me differently."

"Different is unequal in some way?"

"Did you ask me here to debate gender politics or are you going to show me to your study and give me your spiel?"

"The latter." He walked down the marble halls, appreciating the opulence of his home with each step he took. Appreciating that it was his.

He'd spent too many nights on cold cobblestone not to appreciate it. And too many other nights in soft beds that belonged to other people. And honestly, in the end, he wasn't certain the cobblestone wasn't the better option.

The hall opened up into another room with a broad arched doorway, one that reminded him of old buildings in Italy. Places that were far too grand to allow him admittance. So he'd built them for himself, now that he could afford them.

Antique furniture that cost more simply because it was old decorated the room, another possession he'd acquired simply because he could. Same with the marble busts and old vases. Things he'd bought because, before, they were things that museum docents and shopkeepers wouldn't even let him look at.

Now he owned them. Now he owned whatever he wanted. The cost of it had been high enough that he felt entitled to reminders.

Julia sat in the biggest chair in the room, maroon and wingback. She crossed one slim, leather clad leg over the other and leaned back, tapping her patent black stiletto heel on the hard floor.

"Spill it, Calvaresi."

"I want to partner with you and present our plan to Barrows. We can land the account together. And, I have it on good authority, we will easily remove Hamlin from the equation forever if we play our cards right."

"What?"

"To which piece of the statement?"

"All of it. But start with Hamlin."

"He's on the downward slide. He's in so much debt that the only thing that could possibly save Hamlin Tech at this point is a major new account. Barrows. If we don't partner on it, odds are, he gets it. And the bigger picture here, Julia, is not so much you or I getting the account as it is being able to get rid of a key player in our industry."

"That's…well, it's dastardly, is what it is."

"I'd twirl my mustache if I had one," he said, his tone dry.

"I'm serious, why bother to take Hamlin out?"

"Is it your goal to be more successful than him? To steal his customers and cut into his market share?"

"Yes," she said.

"Well, it's my goal, too. It's my goal to do it to you, too, but I can put that on hold because I see an opportunity here. Frankly Hamlin is a bastard, and while I'm not the nicest guy I don't have sweatshops throughout Asia, or harass my female employees."

"So you're just going to play like you're swooping in and saving the world from Hamlin Tech and all the evil it commits?"

"No," he said, crossing his arms over his chest, "but it's another reason he's an enticing target. The main reason is that I want to be the last man standing."

"And why should I enable you to get one step closer to your goal?"

"Because it takes you one step closer, too."

"So we charge in together, then when the enemy is destroyed we turn our weapons on to each other?" She uncrossed her legs and tilted her head to the side, finely groomed eyebrows arched.

"Exactly. Is that a problem?"

"I'm not sure." She folded her hands on her lap and leaned forward, resting her chin on them. She was an interesting woman. All limbs and pale skin and hair, brimming with a kind of uncontainable energy that always seemed to vibrate beneath the surface.

"As long as we're working together, we're working together."

She sucked her bottom lip between her teeth and Ferro felt a strange, answering jolt in his gut. She was a lovely thing.

The sort who had no idea just how lovely. She would need a lot of flattering words, a lot of touch, nonsexual touch, in order to open up. In order to enjoy an encounter with a man.

He mentally castigated himself for the direction of his thoughts. This wasn't the time. And assessing women like that, figuring out what they really wanted, how he might go about fulfilling that, wasn't part of his life anymore.

He hadn't looked at a woman like that in years and he wasn't sure why he did it now. He wasn't after a girlfriend, mistress or woman-for-hire which meant there was no point. It wasn't that he didn't feel attraction, simply that it registered in his body and nowhere else.

Maybe because she was a puzzle. Something about her didn't fit. The energy, for one. She worked so hard to play it down, but she could hardly sit still. Then there was the don't-touch-me black clothes. He imagined they were meant to make her look confident, but in his mind, it only betrayed the fact that she wasn't. She was wearing armor that was far too easy to recognize as such.

But no matter how intriguing, he wasn't going there with her. He would not revert to the man he'd been trained to be. He'd escaped that. He used it when it suited him, not when it didn't. He wasn't on a leash anymore.

"Meaning you won't stab me in the back during this… caper?"

"I wouldn't call it a caper. Although, it will require a bit of…finesse."

"Meaning?"

This was the part she wouldn't like. The part that would have been easy with another woman. But Julia wasn't easy. She didn't respond to his flirtation. Didn't respond to his charm. Charm he knew was lethal in most cases.

But not in this one. Interesting. It made her so very interesting. It always had. No one else went toe-to-toe with him.

No one, not even Scott Hamlin, would dare pull such public stunts the way she did. She'd pushed him to start doing the same. She'd forced him to act. So very interesting to meet someone who had that kind of power.

But it was in his control now.

"We'll have to make it look like our…merging—"

"This is *not* a merger," she bit out.

"For the project," he said.

"Fine," she said, barely civil. "Go on."

"We'll have to make our merging look organic."

"And how do you propose we do that?"

In some ways, the fact that she wasn't going to like his suggestion made it even more perfect. Anything he could do to tip the balance of power further to his favor was only good. And the more flustered she was, the more control he would have. "It would be completely expected for a *couple* to discuss a project and come to the conclusion that collaboration would be the best for all involved."

Her blue eyes glittered. "Are you suggesting that we…that we feign some kind of personal involvement?"

"You're sanitizing it," he said, smiling. "I'm suggesting we pretend we're heavily involved in a scorching affair."

Julia exploded from the chair and started pacing the room. "That's insane. As if I would ever… As if you would… As if… As if!"

"You find the idea so offensive?" He crossed the room and sat in the chair she'd just been occupying.

"I find it unbelievable. After the stunt you pulled today do you really think anyone would believe that you and I…"

"There's a fine line between hate and lust, *cara mia*."

"Maybe if you have a disconnect between your brain and your nether regions."

"And many people do."

She looked down, then back up, hands planted on her hips. "That's crazy."

"Do you have a better idea? Why should Barrows have any confidence in our ability to work together if we present a proposal out of the blue?"

She flung her hands wide. "Because we're awesome!"

"Awesome doesn't score points in business, Julia, and this is where being like me has an advantage over being like you."

"*Like me* as in young, extremely smart, creative and—"

"Green. Untried. Untrained."

"And what about you, Ferro Calvaresi, graduate of the school of hard knocks?"

No, she wasn't a woman to win over with seduction. But when she was challenged? She couldn't resist fighting back. "Hard knocks? Have you been reading my unauthorized bio?"

Color stained her cheeks, crimson against the pale white of her skin. "No. It's a common expression."

"And it's also in the front jacket of the book. My rise to success from the seedy underbelly of Rome. Fantastic reading. If you like a fairy tale."

It was almost amusing that she, along with the rest of the world, had jumped at the chance to read about his sordid past. And it was sordid, no mistake, no denying. A good thing for him, the book only scratched the surface. Sure there were whispers, whispers that were close to the truth, but no one really knew.

"I have no idea what book you're talking about."

"I think you do, but you can have your lie."

She was all but bouncing in place now, her knee flexing in time with something in her head. Probably the horrible names she was silently calling him. "Fine. I read it. Know your enemy and all. *The Art of War.* See? I'm on top of stuff."

"It's like your mommy and daddy got you a CEO boxed

set for Christmas. Did you also get a world's best boss mug and a zen garden?"

"Make your point, or I walk," she bit out.

"My point is that you've had success easy and young." She bit her lip, like she was holding back words she wanted desperately to speak. Words that would be designed to castrate him, of that he had no doubt. "Because of that success, you've never had to deal with the realities of setbacks. Of how business works. Of the nuances of it. You didn't have to court the press, they came to you. You haven't had to turn scandal around and make it work to your advantage. Haven't had to twist lies around so that they're close enough to the truth no one will examine it all too closely, but I have. I know what we're dealing with here. I know the manner of man Scott Hamlin really is, and I won't hesitate to take him out completely."

"You say that like I don't know that manner of man," she said, her tone frosty. "I'm a woman in a man's world. Tech is a boys' club, Calvaresi. There's practically a No Girls Allowed sign on the door. I've been dealing with men all my life who want to take from me, who think they can just take from women. I do know about men like Hamlin. And you're right. He deserves nothing less than total professional destruction."

"He would do nothing less to us. He's tried to, or didn't you know?"

"What?"

"You look shocked."

"I am. He's never tried to do anything to me."

"You think not? Well, he's the man who's seventy percent responsible for my unauthorized bio, which you are familiar with. And he's also responsible for the IRS rechecking all of your returns last year."

"How did you know about that?"

"It's getting tiresome but I'll say it again. Corporate espionage." He watched her expression change, watched her skin turn a deeper pink. He really had made her angry now.

"Who do you have in my company?"

"Who says I have anyone in there? Now."

"Ferro…"

"I never confirm anything. I don't deny it, either, so you might as well not waste your time trying to get either from me."

"Fine. So you say he's trying to take us down."

"Yes. And if you were more scandalous he may have succeeded."

She frowned. "Excuse me? You're extremely scandalous and he didn't succeed with you."

Ferro shrugged. "Because I know how to play it."

"Is this where 'neither confirm nor deny' comes in?"

"Absolutely. My point is, Julia, you need to play this my way. Because while I appreciate that you're a tech wunderkind—"

"I'm twenty-five. I'm not that young."

Nearly ten years his junior, and even younger when it came to life experience. Julia didn't look tired yet. But she would. Life had a way of doing that to people. Especially people thrust into the spotlight.

Lucky for him, in many ways, he'd come in worn down and tired. And at least now he had a bed that belonged to him.

"You are young," he said. "And the fact that you don't realize it only highlights that fact. And while that is its own kind of amazing, its own achievement, it is not what I have. Maturity."

"You? Ferro Calvaresi? You're playing the maturity card? You just…hijacked my presentation like a…a…pillaging tech pirate and now you're trying to tell me you're mature?"

He gave her his most practiced smile, smooth, genuine,

a smile no one could find fault with. A smile he never felt at all. "I show the world what I choose to show the world."

"You think I don't?"

"I think your armor is thin, *cara.*"

He expected her to make some sort of snitty denial. Say she didn't wear armor. She didn't, and that was to her credit.

"You tell me then," she said, slowly crossing her arms beneath her breasts, her blue eyes never wavering from his, "what do you think we need to do?"

"We need to make the world believe that all of our hostility has melted away into an attraction, an attachment, that we can't deny. We need to make them think we've fallen head over heels into, if not love, bed."

"And you think that will work?" She was blushing. He couldn't remember ever seeing a woman blush. Or anyone for that matter. Everyone he'd ever known had seemed born jaded.

He hadn't been. He could remember a time when he'd been young. When he'd felt hope. Optimism. Passion.

He'd learned. He'd learned that there were no bonus points for getting through life without mud on your hands. Sometimes you had to get dirty climbing out of the gutter, but at least you were out, even if the filth clung to your skin for the rest of your life. Even if it made you hard and old before your time.

"I know it will."

"How?"

"The press, the public, are predictable. We show up at a public event, we'll make headlines around the world. The seed will be planted, when we pitch our design to Barrows, it all suddenly makes sense."

She flicked her hair back over her shoulder and shifted her weight, one stiletto clad foot out in front of her. "But won't Hamlin see it coming?"

"Not necessarily. I said it would make sense. I didn't say it would be predictable. I'm banking on his own ignorance to be his downfall in this. He would never partner with a woman. He'll assume I won't, either."

She chewed her bottom lip, another show of that insecurity she kept concealed by all her hard black clothing. If this were a seduction, he would touch her face now. Just her cheek. Tell her it would be all right. She would respond to that.

He gritted his teeth. "Well? You were quick to remind me you had limited time, Julia. I am a man with many commitments and I can't stand around waiting for you to make a decision that should be a very easy one to make."

She extended her hand and he gripped it. She was so petite, fine-boned, her fingers long, slender and clinging to his with a firmness that surprised him. She was indeed a businesswoman.

"You have yourself a deal, Calvaresi."

"Gratified to hear it, Anderson."

"We work together on this project," she said. "No touching that isn't strictly necessary, no funny ideas about things heating up behind the scenes, and no espionage."

The espionage happening in her company was well in place, information already being fed to him on a regular basis. And he was sure she'd done the same to him. Fair play during their normal operations.

This agreement changed things. But he imagined as long as he didn't look at it during the duration of their agreement, it would count as him following the rules. Or maybe not. But he'd never been one for rules. "I think I can handle all of the above."

"And when it's over, it's over. If I have a chance to get you in my crosshairs even thirty seconds after our work together is done, I'll do it and I'll pull the metaphorical trigger without hesitation."

"Back at you," he said, releasing his hold and dropping his hand back at his side, ignoring the slight burning sensation that skated over his skin.

"Until then, I suppose we have to play nice."

Ferro smiled, and he watched the color in Julia's cheeks darken again. "Now that, I can't promise. I'm not all that nice."

CHAPTER THREE

"ARE YOU BUSY tonight?"

Julia frowned as she heard the voice that was coming over her personal cell phone. "How did you get this—oh, never mind. Let me guess, you crawled through the ducting in the building and rappelled down over my desk and hunted until you found my phone, then you stole the number and went back the way you came."

"No. What a waste of energy. I called and got it from your assistant."

Julia glared daggers at Thad through the wall. "Why would he do that?"

"He assumed that a call from me would be important. And since I am now your lover—" the way he said the word made Julia's skin feel prickly "—I will of course need to contact you day and night."

She hated that he was right. She hated that she'd agreed to all this in the first place, but she really, really wanted the Barrows deal and if she had to make a deal with the devil to get it, well, she was willing.

Not happily willing, but willing. Once the account was landed, Ferro wouldn't be her problem. It wasn't as though they'd be working closely together on the creation of the navigation system, not after the initial design phase.

She could survive him. She could deal. At least in this she

had control. It wasn't like being dressed up in the world's most horrific prom dress and being sent off with a guy who was being paid to be your date. No, she had a stake in this. She had power. This was all about the big picture and, regardless of what he thought, she understood business.

"Right, right. And why did you need to know if I was busy?"

"I was wondering if you might like to go to a movie premiere with me."

"A premiere? For what?"

"*Cold Planet* is coming out tonight, and I have an invitation for Ferro Calvaresi and Guest."

For a second, she forgot to play cool. She forgot who she was talking to. "No way! That movie looks amazing."

"You think?"

"It's like every sci-fi dream from my childhood come to life on the big screen!" It was too late to pull back her over-enthusiastic words. She was always doing things like this to herself, even now that she'd been coached on how to behave in public by professionals.

Normal people didn't get so excited about movies. Geeks did. It made people uncomfortable, and no one else was really that interested. That was what her mother had told her. Daily. From the time she was a five-year-old girl who talked about how she wanted to make the navigation controls on a spaceship from a futuristic movie and put them into cars someday.

She'd been embarrassing for her parents. Rattling on about strange subjects constantly, no filter for her excitement and enthusiasm. Making her normal had been her mother's lifelong goal. She'd wanted it enough that she'd bought Julia a prom date when she'd been sixteen.

That had been the end of it. The end of trying to be normal. But she'd learned something even more important that night. There was no protection in normal. But showing who you were? Making yourself vulnerable? That was the biggest mistake of all.

She'd come out of that night, that horrible night, stronger. And when she'd taken off that ridiculous pink dress, the one she'd spent hours choosing, she'd put armor on instead. Armor she'd been wearing ever since. On that, Ferro was right. She didn't really like that Ferro was right.

Still, even with the armor she had some rough edges to smooth out. She tried hard not to wave that geek flag too high. Not anymore. She had a public face that was so much more socially acceptable, and it helped her get by in the media without having to take too many pot shots.

Which was fine with her. She'd had quite enough growing up.

Stupid bitch, I was doing you a favor. No other guy will ever touch you.

She shook off the memory. It didn't matter. Those words, the touch of his hands, the way they seemed to linger, didn't matter. She'd moved on. Moved forward. She'd kept her head down and worked hard, free from caring what anyone thought, not after all that.

It was why she'd succeeded. And with all her money, she'd hired her consultants, consultants who'd helped make her look like a kick-ass video game heroine, who'd helped her learn to speak with poise and confidence.

She wasn't vulnerable now. And while Giddy Excited Julia was allowed to jump around inside of her over movies and games, she was not allowed out to play.

"Well," he said, "I happened to have provided some of the software used for the highly sophisticated special effects, which landed me with the invite."

She closed the door on her memories and focused on the presents. "Right, I was a little jealous about that."

"But you don't have the tech for this sort of thing."

"No. I make technology for regular people," she said, swiveling her chair in a circle. "Anyway, I really get to come?" She would go chained to Ferro's leg if she had to. It was way too fun to pass up. She would go even if they weren't partnering on the Barrows deal together.

"Yes. Formal dress. Though, it is a sci-fi film, if you wanted to do a gold bikini and a slave collar, I think that would be acceptable attire."

"Har, har, Calvaresi. Anyway, that's *Star Wars*. *Cold Planet* is an entirely different mythology. It's based off of this first-person shooter game and…" She clamped her mouth shut. She was doing it again. "And I'm hardly going to a public event in a costume."

"You'll have to tell me more about mythologies at the premiere."

She was sure he was making fun of her. She basically deserved it at this point. It was one thing to get in front of a room full of people and make a scripted speech, but still, even still, social interaction had the potential to be painfully awkward. She was out of practice. If she'd ever been in-practice.

"Sure," she said. "What time?"

"I'll pick you up at five. We have to walk the carpet, then we get to view the movie."

"Wow." So a lot more social interaction on the docket. Goody. "Neat."

"You sound thrilled."

"About the movie, yes."

"Great, see you at five." He hung up and she leaned back in her chair. Then she scrambled forward and hit the intercom on her phone. "Thad."

"Yes?" Her assistant's voice came through the speaker.

"I need a dress. A hot one. Get Ally on it, please. And I need to get my hair done."

"Formal? And by when?"

"Yes, and I need to be waiting out front of the building at four-fifty."

Thad sighed heavily. She knew she was asking the next-to impossible, but she also knew if anyone could get it arranged, it was him. "As you wish."

"Great. Thank you. You rock. I have to go." She pushed the off button and rested her chin on her desk, her hands on her lap. Then she took a breath and straightened. She was going to be fine. She wasn't going to think about how ill-equipped she was to show up at a Hollywood premiere on the arm of a man like Ferro. She wasn't going to think about how likely it was that she would drop a shrimp cocktail into her cleavage during the party.

No. She was going to sit back and let the professionals she hired to make her camera-ready do what they did best. If nothing else, she would look good. She would look strong.

Money might not buy happiness, but it bought an image that made it possible for her to go out in public.

And yes, she was Ferro's date. But it wasn't a date-date. Thank God. The last time she'd had a date it had been an un-mitigated disaster. And *that* guy hadn't been Ferro sex-on-a-cracker Calvaresi.

Not that she was all that familiar with sex. On a cracker or otherwise. But Ferro was. Her face got hot when she thought of some of the more revealing parts of Ferro's unauthorized bio. Yes, she'd read it. And it made it hard to look the man in the eye.

He wasn't just hot. He was the kind of man who made women lose their minds. Who inspired respectable members of society to throw off the bonds of convention and flaunt him at social gatherings. He'd been the much-younger stud of a few women back in his home country, setting off scandalous headlines and dissolving marriages.

Of course, that was assuming that version of his life was

true. And that was assuming a lot. And as Ferro had said, he never confirmed or denied.

She took another fortifying breath. Great. Fine. She could do this. Tonight, she was going to be yet another rumor to add to Ferro's list. And she wouldn't confirm or deny.

When Ferro's limo pulled up to the curb in front of Julia's high-rise, he was genuinely stunned by her appearance. She was utterly captivating in a long black dress—the woman didn't seem to own another color—that skimmed the gray sidewalk. The sleeves were long and full, like a kimono, and the neck high, revealing very little of her pale skin.

Her blond hair was pulled back in a low, messy bun, her makeup done all in shades of pale pink and gold. Her lips were painted the lightest rose, and it created the strangest curiosity in him. A fascination with what they might look like darker, flushed with arousal. Strange because he never felt curious about those things. He knew all about sex. There was no mystery left.

He'd opened the door and let her into the limo, and then both of them had spent the drive down the interstate on their mobile devices, finishing up the day's interrupted work.

When they pulled up to Grauman's Chinese Theatre, the streets were already blocked off. Ferro's limo was given immediate access, and they were let out near the end of the red carpet. This sort of thing had never been his favorite aspect of fame. The fortune was his biggest draw. These events did very little for him. Giving fake smiles to even faker people ranked low on his list of things he'd like to do with his Friday night.

Julia had the most purposeful look of boredom on her face he'd ever seen. Like she was forcing her lips to stay pulled together, forcing herself not to smile. She was stiff, walking with her head held high, her posture overly straight.

But beneath all of that, she was vibrating under the surface. Energy was pouring from her in waves, though he knew no one standing far away from her would ever be able to tell. But he could feel her shaking.

She seemed to like a spectacle, her presentations were so ostentatious it was unreal, but then, she was in control of them. The press played by her rules in those situations. Perhaps that was the cause of her unease now. It wasn't her security keeping the fans at bay. The press weren't being held to her guidelines.

He pulled her to him, lacing his fingers through hers. "We're ready to walk the carpet." He could feel her fingers trembling in his. "Relax," he said. "We aren't the A list. We won't be mobbed."

"I've seen pictures snapped of you while you were getting coffee at Roasted. You're mobbed frequently."

"Yes, but not when there are movie stars around. Come on. Anyway, if we are mobbed, our purposes will be served even better." He tugged her along and when they stepped onto the carpet, he turned his smile on full.

Julia did the same, waving at the crowd lining the velvet rope that partitioned the masses from the golden few, hand-selected to enter into the realm of the elite. Very often Ferro felt like he still had more in common with those behind the rope.

She walked a bit ahead of him, her steps nervous and quick, and that was when he noticed the back of her dress, or rather, the lack of it, for the first time. It was cut low and wide, a swath of white skin on show from her shoulder blades down to the indent of her back, just above the curve of her butt.

It was the shock of it that made him want to touch. He was sure of that. He was a man far too jaded by his past to be aroused by a wedge of skin. Far too jaded to allow himself to be aroused at all, unless it was late at night and he needed a sleep aid. And yet, he found that he was. That fascinated him nearly as much as her exposed skin.

"Slow down," he said, pulling her back to his side.

"Sorry," she said, a smile still plastered on her face. "Nervous."

"Don't be. Just remember, they're all here to see you. You're the one in the enviable position. You're beautiful. Successful. Everyone out there would love to be here. They would trade places with you in a heartbeat." The words came, easy and without much thought or sincerity. He was good at giving compliments. At giving women exactly what they desired.

At keeping his mind somewhere else entirely, even while he gave all of his body. A perfect disconnect.

Her smile altered subtly, became more genuine. "That was a nice thing to say."

"It's true," he said, without pausing to think if it really was.

"Ferro! Julia!"

Julia's head whipped around in the direction of her name. She noticed that Ferro kept his movements much less spastic, kept his emotions better hidden. But she was having a much harder time with it. She'd trained herself to keep her reactions and emotions much more veiled than this, but she'd never been to a movie premiere before. And this movie premiere was a fangirl paradise, which, she admittedly was.

Back before she'd decided being herself wasn't worth the pain, she would have been lining the streets with the crowd. Probably wearing some kind of Space Fleet Academy uniform.

The flashbulbs were directed at them now and she just smiled and hoped, feverishly, that she didn't have leftovers from lunch in her teeth or a false eyelash stuck to her cheek or anything similarly horrifying.

Ferro, for his part, was immaculate in his dark suit and tie, short hair in perfect order. The man simply never looked anything less than composed and pressed. She'd bet he didn't go home and put on a gigantic sweater and yoga pants after a long day of work. He probably wore a black silk robe and... nothing underneath.

She nearly choked.

"Are you on a date?" one of the reporters shouted over the din.

Ferro simply smiled and said, "If you have to ask, perhaps I'm doing it wrong."

Jeez. The man oozed charm. She'd never seen him not at ease. Even when she'd pulled off her great OnePhone caper and messed with his product launch, his public face had remained completely smooth.

"Julia, any comments?"

"We better be. I don't want to have to pay for my own dinner." That earned her some laughter and she was gratified that she'd managed a witty response. Especially since half of her brainpower was being used up to focus on the heat that was coursing from her palm, where Ferro was holding her hand, up her arm, to her breasts, making her nipples, of all things, tingle a little bit.

Ferro waved and she did the same, and they walked on, into the ornate theater where they were ushered to their seats. Ferro released her as soon as they were in the dark.

And again, Julia felt like she was in danger of getting whiplash from the recognizable faces surrounding them. "I think that's—"

"Don't stare, Julia, it's rude."

She shot Ferro a deadly glare he probably couldn't see in the darkness. "Sorry. I forgot we were being blasé." And she shouldn't have forgotten. Anything else was way too revealing and embarrassing.

"You'll get to the point where you don't have to remember. Trust me."

"You think?" she asked, looking sideways at him in the dark.

"I know. You're lucky life hasn't knocked it out of you yet."

She leaned back in her chair. "You have no idea what life has taken from me," she said. For the second time in the same day, she thought back to that long-ago prom night. Why was she thinking about it so much? She never thought about it. She'd moved on from it. She was fine. Bruises healed. And the stuff that didn't? It had helped her realize that you had to be strong. It had been when she'd stopped trying to fit in, when she'd stopped being so afraid to be unusual. She'd just started owning it then. And it had been the key to her success.

She wasn't sending out any thank-you cards to the jackass who'd assaulted her, but she wasn't wallowing, either.

"I'd venture to say you know less about mine than you think you do, Julia," he said, his words darker than the theater.

"I read the bio," she said.

He chuckled, a sound that lacked humor and warmth. "As I said, you know less about me than you think. Just because it's in print, doesn't mean it's the whole truth."

The End of the Tech World As We Know It?

The headline screamed up at Julia from the newspaper, just delivered to her tablet. Ferro was already in her office, sitting in the chair in front of her desk like he had every right to be there.

"Not exactly the headline we anticipated," he said.

"Ya think?" She skimmed the article, her stomach sinking. "Either a sharp blow to progress or a cheap publicity stunt," she read out loud.

"Because if we're sleeping together we won't be competing, and if we aren't competing, will we be on our game?"

"I have a lot of words rolling around in my head right now and they're all filthy," she said, standing up and pacing up and down in front of her office window. "What are we going to do? It's everywhere. It's trending on Twitter. There's a Facebook page, Calvaresi, a freaking Facebook page devoted to... what are they calling us?" She leaned in and skimmed the article again. "JulErro. For the love of Darth."

"And for everyone rooting for this little enemies-to-lovers tale…"

"There are just as many rooting for us to go down in flames. This…this is a lot bigger than we anticipated, isn't it?"

Ferro wished he could say he'd anticipated just this, but the simple fact was, social media was hard to anticipate. The press was one thing, the civilian-run news machine? Something else entirely. And the simple truth was, this had gone way outside the tech world, thanks to the internet, which was run by the masses. Who were entirely unpredictable.

"Yes," he said. "It is."

The feeling of claustrophobia he felt now, the feeling of being trapped, he didn't like it. A trap of his own making. And it wasn't the first one he'd ever been in. He knew all about this. About going so far down a road there was no way to turn back. That you just had to push through, keep going, because you'd gone too damn far.

"Fine," she said, continuing to pace. "We continue on, and we make it the biggest spectacle ever. And when we blow it up, we make it huge. The biggest media explosion ever. And we'll always be more interesting after this. Think about it, when you hijack another one of my presentations, just think how newsworthy it will be when we're exes? Hypothetically. Don't hijack one of my presentations again."

Julia might be wearing armor, but she was a tough woman. Smart. Brilliant even. "Of course," he said, "we'll be expected to spend a lot of time together. A lot. The visibility is too high. We're going to have to give them something to talk about, because if we don't…if we get caught in this…"

"We're in trouble."

"Putting it mildly."

"Okay…okay…what's the plan then?"

"There's a charity event tonight. I was planning on skipping it and writing a check, but I think we should make an appearance, don't you? As a couple."

Julia looked like she was going to say something, but she hesitated.

"Come on, Julia," he said. "Don't wimp out now."

"I'm not wimping out!"

"Then why do you look like a deer caught in the headlights?"

"Because the other day we were sworn enemies and if I never had to see you in person it suited me just fine. Now… two outings with you in a row? I could live without that."

"Maybe this is why tech, and business in general, is traditionally a man's game," he said, not meaning a word he was saying but knowing it would give Julia the kick she needed. "Maybe it's because women are too ruled by emotion."

He knew it wasn't true. Because he'd been…he didn't even know what to call it. Shaped, molded, by women who hadn't cared what their actions meant to the emotions of a teenage boy. He'd spent years surrounded by women who saw people only as pawns. People of both genders were more than capable of acting based on selfish desire. Of using people to meet their ends.

But his words would push Julia. He knew it. Knew it was a hot button for her.

"Are you saying I can't do this?" she asked.

"You're the one who looks like she has a problem. I'm willing to make this work. Are you? Or are you just giving me lip service here?"

She narrowed her eyes. "I'm going to ignore the potential double entendre there."

"If it suits you."

"Fine. You have yourself a date for tonight. Ferro?"

"Yes?"

"Uh…what's the charity?" He had a feeling that wasn't the question she'd intended to ask.

"For homeless youths."

"Great. I'll bring my checkbook."

CHAPTER FOUR

CHARITY EVENTS WERE the scourge of Ferro's existence. A shiny, gorgeous hotel ballroom, filled with internally ugly people who possessed an unnatural amount of self-importance. People who manipulated and used the less fortunate for their own pleasure during the day, but showed up to things like this to show their altruism to the press.

He could well remember the first time he'd been in a room like this. Hating who he was with. Hating that he had to smile and fawn and do whatever it was he'd been paid to do. No matter whether he wanted it. No. The tabloids, the author of his bio, they really had no idea of the depths he'd been to.

He looked at Julia, who was holding on to his arm like it was a live eel, the smile on her face anything but easy, and he wondered if he had become no better.

No. This benefitted Julia, too. It was an exchange.

Like sex for money?

Hell, no. This wasn't the same.

Why was he even thinking about it? He rarely did. But it happened more since Julia and he had struck their unholy alliance. No one knew the truth. They believed, of course, that he'd slept his way to the top. He'd been spotted with some very wealthy older women in his younger years. But they didn't know the truth.

The rumors clung to him, disgusted him. Because of the

ring of truth to them. But he would walk the same path a thousand times to end up where he was today. He just went on, proving his right to be in his position with his continued success.

Regret was for the weak. And he wasn't wasting any time on it tonight. Or ever. He was shutting it off. The way he'd shut off the feelings of bone deep hunger and cold he'd experienced as a child on the street. The way he'd shut down the shame and pain when he'd been lifted up from that gutter where he'd been and brought into a glittering, hideous world that had asked for his soul in exchange for food and a warm bed. In exchange for eventual success.

The way he shut desire down now, to avoid ever thinking about that time in his life.

Tonight, for this, he would shut off what little conscience he had left, and go forward. Because it was the best thing to do. Because the end always justified the means. Always. And because he was no longer the boy he'd once been. He was the man with the power. And that meant he would win in the end.

As they moved through the room, a wave of whispers followed. Everyone was watching them. Everyone was interested.

"Try to relax," he said to Julia.

"I am relaxed."

"Which leads me to the conclusion that you genuinely don't know how to relax. You're tense. You're practically shivering."

She looked down at her hands. "I have a lot of energy."

"Is that so? Then perhaps we should put it to good use." He shifted his hold on her and laced their fingers together, drawing her out toward the high gloss dance floor.

"Why?" she asked, her tone petulant.

"Why what?"

"Why the dancing?" She looked genuinely worried now, all that tough-chick bravado gone.

"Because the headline will be sensational." He drew her up against his body and felt her frame tremble beneath his touch. It wasn't attraction. He was well familiar with women being attracted to him. She looked...scared. "I'm not going to bite you," he said.

"I know." She looked around. "But I'm going to look stupid."

"Follow my lead."

He began to step in time with the music, guiding Julia's movements. She clung to his shoulder, her nails digging into him through the fabric of his jacket. He was familiar with that, with long nails pressed into his skin, a memory from his past. But this, again, was different.

She stumbled, the heel of her shoe harsh on his toe, even with his custom leather shoes to cushion the blow. Her face turned pink. "Sorry."

"It's fine." He kept on moving, and she stumbled again, the color in her cheeks deepening.

"This isn't really my thing," she said, looking over his shoulder, at the people behind them. "People are staring."

"Most of them probably like our Facebook page. We're infamous now, not just famous."

"Weren't you already?"

He smiled. "Yes. Welcome to the dark side."

"I'm not sure I like that I've joined you here."

"So, you've always kept your conscience clean before your association with me?"

She looked down. "Of course."

"Do I make you feel dirty, Julia?"

She lifted her head, her eyes round, face pink. He'd succeeded in shocking. In putting her off balance. He didn't know why he needed to do it. To prove that he was still in control?

Maybe. The control felt tenuous with her in his arms, her skin soft beneath the palm of his hand.

But this was just a game. Like every other sexual game he'd ever played. He had a part to play. It had nothing to do with him, with what he wanted. It didn't even matter what she wanted. It mattered what the press wanted to see.

And they wanted a show. A show he was going to make sure they got.

"Every association I've ever had with you has made me feel like I had a little dirt on my hands now that you mention it."

"I'd ask you how it feels to sell your soul for money. But I already know."

Her eyes widened, her mouth dropping open. She looked so…sweet. Not in personality, but like her flavor would be that of a fine dessert. He wondered.

Hell, he didn't have to wonder. It was time to put on the show. Not because he was wondering about her lips, but because he couldn't have her standing there, staring at him with a guppylike expression on her face.

He stopped, then put his hand on her cheek. Her skin was soft. Warm. Then he leaned in, and she stiffened, just a bit, beneath his touch. "Come with me to the terrace. It's much more private." He moved his hand up and down her back in a smooth, lingering caress before releasing her from his hold and taking them both off the dance floor, across the room and out the doors that led to the secluded balcony that overlooked the ocean.

"What are you doing?" she snapped when they were outside.

"I'm sparing you the dancing embarrassment, and giving the public what they want. What's better than being seen on the dance floor? Being seen sneaking off of it for a little privacy." He looked back in the ballroom and noticed that their movements had been followed by a woman who was now watching them far too closely to be mistaken for a casual observer. "We already have the attention of the paparazzi. And, if I'm not mistaken, a woman taking pictures with a OnePhone."

"Ten points to me."

He took a step toward her and she retreated, her back butting against the stucco wall of the hotel. "Kiss me," he said.

"What?"

"We're out here on a darkened terrace, there is only one possible reason for such a move."

"Is that so?"

"Yes. I want you. I can't keep my hands off you, and I had to remove us from civilized company so I could give in to my fantasies and have my way with you."

"Oh?"

"Yes. Julia, the only thing that could push two storied rivals into each other's arms is the kind of lust that doesn't follow the rules. A kind of passion that defies logic and reason. The kind that would see us rushing off the dance floor to somewhere we could be alone."

Julia's mouth and throat had gone completely dry. No man, ever, had looked at her with the kind of intensity Ferro was focusing on her now.

Her prom date, Michael, had viewed her with a weird sort of anger and aggression. Even as he'd been forcing kisses on her, it hadn't been because of lust or attraction, but some need to dominate. To own her.

The attempted rape had had nothing to do with him wanting her sexually. He'd been violent. Hateful and insulting. Frightening.

Ferro wasn't looking at her like that. He was all heat and interest, intensity. Desire. Like he was looking at her, really looking at her. And the thing was, she knew it was part of the game. She knew that Ferro turned the charm on and off like a tap, that he had all this down to an art.

He was a legendary lover. According to the book, women had risked all just to be with him. To feel his touch. To be in his bed. She could almost understand.

He extended his hand, traced the line of her jaw, to her chin with his index finger. "Kiss me, Julia."

"What if I don't want to?" she asked. "I don't even like you."

A smile curved his lips. "You don't have to like someone to want them."

"I do."

"Think about all the times I've messed with your plans, all the times my new computer system outsold your new computer system. And think about how badly you wanted to slap my face. Think of me interrupting your presentation. Now I want you to channel all that into your kiss. Do you understand?"

She was trembling. Honest to goodness, her lips were trembling. And her heart was about to burst through her chest.

He leaned in, his lips brushing her ear, his breath hot on her neck. "Think of how angry I make you. And then kiss me like it's my punishment." He let his finger drift to her bottom lip, traced the outline of her mouth.

His words shivered through her body, a spark that crackled along her veins. And he made her forget that she'd just tripped all over him on the dance floor. He made her forget about kisses that had hurt and bruised. He made her forget she was ridiculously inexperienced for a woman her age. He made her forget everything but the desire to follow his instructions exactly.

And he even made it feel like it was her idea.

Because she wanted it. Wanted this. How had he made her want it? She didn't even care.

The entire ruse they were engaged in depended on the fact that the heat of passion that came from hate could easily be ignited into attraction. And right now, it felt so very true.

She put her hand on the back of his neck, her palm tingling as it came into contact with his skin. It had been a long time since she'd kissed anyone. She just hoped she remembered how it went.

Then she leaned forward and pressed her lips to his and realized it didn't matter if she remembered how to kiss, because this wasn't anything like the other kisses she'd experienced.

She did think of him interrupting her presentation. Of the times he'd sent her asinine "memos" designed to taunt her with his success. And that, combined with the press of his lips against hers, built a fire in her blood that she was afraid might burn out of control.

She clung to him, her fingers laced through his hair, her hold firm. He braced himself, one hand on the wall behind him, his other arm moving to wrap tightly around her waist, pulling her up against his hard, muscular body.

He angled his head, deepened the kiss, his tongue sliding over hers. There was no way a photographer could see that. He was getting way too into character.

But she found she didn't much care. Especially when she dipped her tongue into his mouth, tasted him, then bit down hard on his bottom lip. His punishment, as requested.

She most especially didn't care when that move brought on a deep, feral growl that rumbled through his body, made his kiss intensify.

She arched into him, pressed her breasts against his chest. Until she couldn't think anymore. Until everything, the anger, the confusion, the deception, dissolved into one big blur of desperation and passion that eclipsed everything else.

She felt the almost-unshakable urge to move her hands from his hair, down his shoulders, to his chest. Just to see what muscles like that would feel like beneath her palms. To know what it was like to touch a man who was so perfectly formed.

She didn't, though. Mostly because she was afraid if she shifted their positions in any way, she would lose her grip on him and slowly sink down into a puddle.

When he lifted his head, she felt like she'd run a marathon, and she wasn't sure if she would ever be able to catch her breath.

"That," he said, "should be sufficient. I think it will leave little doubt about our personal involvement. And I'm certain it's been caught on camera."

"Oh." It was all she could say. Her brain had completely shorted out about the time he'd put his tongue in her mouth.

"And even better, it's a completely appropriate time for us to leave, since we've just shown we have other things on our minds."

"Right."

"Everything okay?"

"Fine. It just seems like we just got here and…and I have to write a check."

"We have work in the morning."

"I know."

"I forgot, you never run out of energy."

Except she felt oddly tired now. And more than a little unnerved. She wasn't sure why she'd responded to him the way that she had. Yes, he was a good kisser, but women were supposed to be more cerebral about these things. The mind was supposed to be her gender's largest sexual organ. Which meant the whole not-liking-him thing should have mattered. Should have affected her enjoyment of the kiss. And yet, it didn't. If anything, it fueled the excitement of it.

It was strange especially because of her past experience with sex and anger. But this felt…completely different.

Even so, it seemed weird that she liked it so much. But her feelings for him had never been neutral, so of course, kissing him wouldn't make her feel neutral.

And she was a woman, after all. She wasn't immune to sexy men. Like Thad. He was hot, and she had definitely noticed. If she was Thad's type who knows? She might have indulged in a little fling with her personal assistant. Maybe. If the idea of trying to seduce a guy didn't make her sweaty and nervous.

She hadn't had time to be sweaty and nervous with Ferro because her brain had been nonfunctioning. But it was starting to function a little better, and the nerves were definitely coming.

"Right. Yeah. Late nights don't really bother me."

"Me, either, it was just an excuse. I'm not especially fond of these kinds of events."

"Why is that?"

His expression went ice-cold, hard, his lips, sensual before, thinned into a flat line. "Old memories. The past has never been my favorite place."

It was the first time she'd seen him falter. Sure, she'd made him angry before, but even then, he'd had control over what he'd displayed.

The chill that came over him now wasn't anything like what she'd seen of him before. It seemed more real. And a whole lot scarier.

"Right, well, me, either. High school basically sucked. I had braces and zits and these really thick glasses…"

"Sounds like it was tough," he said, clearly not of the opinion that it was. "But it's time to go."

But he had no idea. No idea what it was like to feel like an outsider, not just in school, but at home. To have your mother pay a guy behind your back to be your date. And to have that date…that date that still had a twenty from your mom in his wallet, try to force you into sex, then hit you when you said no.

No, he didn't know about that. And he didn't need to. It didn't matter anyway. Because now she understood, understood that normal wasn't so shiny and perfect. That normal and "functional" didn't really mean anything at all. Because somehow everyone had thought that a guy who would try to rape his date was normal, while those same people were convinced something was wrong with her.

It hadn't left her with much confidence in people.

She nodded slowly and he looped his arm through hers. They went back into the ballroom and she felt like all eyes were on them, which they doubtlessly were. They'd just very conspicuously gone out to the balcony for fifteen minutes, and now Ferro was rushing them through the crowd at a speed that spoke of urgency.

Oh, yes, they had earned the stares.

She'd never been big in the dating scene, so it was an interesting experience being on the arm of a guy like Ferro.

Well, since becoming a billionaire she'd had more than a few guys after her, but they were all the same. Gorgeous, dumb, lazy and in possession of very little knowledge of the *Lord of the Rings* trilogy. In short, totally worthless to her.

But they didn't count. They didn't even have the decency to want her for her body. Just her money. And that wasn't exactly a turn-on.

Of course, her for-show kiss with Ferro should not have been a turn-on, but darned if she wasn't just a little on the turned-on side of things. Pulse racing, breasts aching. Yeah, turned on, for sure.

She hoped her heated cheeks weren't as pink as she was imagining them, and followed Ferro out of the ballroom and to the front of the hotel, where his limo was already waiting.

"Nice work, Calvaresi—texted your driver did you?"

"I have an app that lets me send down a brief alert when I need to be picked up. It even gives my location to the driver. Just in case over the course of the evening I wind up in a different place than where he dropped me off."

She got in, and Ferro slid in beside her. "Oh, like if you bar hop or something?"

His smile turned naughty. "Or something."

Oh. Yes. That. The going back to a random hotel with a random woman. Strange, considering the reputation Ferro had as a legendary lover, that he wasn't actually photographed with women all that often.

She frowned. "Right."

"Now, don't look jealous, *cara,* those other women, they meant nothing." He wasn't being sincere. He wasn't even trying to look sincere, and yet her body, her heart, which, she swore skipped a beat, didn't seem to care.

She leaned back in her seat and crossed her arms. All the better to keep from reaching out and touching him again. "It's almost frightening how full of crap you are."

"Excuse me?"

"The smile." She punctuated that with a wide, cheesy grin of her own. "The pickup lines. You're very good at it, Ferro. It's easy to forget that it's all a show and you're just a big empty husk of a man with no heart and no soul."

"Ah, you see right through me," he said, still smiling, still looking at her like she was the only woman on earth. "I would advise you to remember the words you just said to me, because you may need them later. I am a man with little in the way of a conscience and it would do you well to keep that in mind."

"Don't worry, Ferro, I won't forget. I'm not in the habit of trusting men. Anyone, really. I won't lapse with you."

But with his dark eyes trained on hers, and the impression of his mouth still burned into her lips, she was afraid that if she didn't watch herself, she would be tempted to forget. Just so she could enjoy the fantasy of the man.

Because the fantasy of him was more compelling than any reality she'd had yet, at least in terms of kissing and desire.

But the important thing to remember was that it was a fantasy. Was that this was a tentative alliance at best. And that when all of the deceit was stripped away, when this night was nothing more than a memory, Ferro Calvaresi was her deadliest enemy.

And that was much more important than a kiss. No matter how scorching.

CHAPTER FIVE

JULIA HUFFED OUT a curse word as the doors to the elevator opened. She'd been in her office, ready to start the day with a tureen of coffee, when Ferro had called, demanding her presence at his office. No, he wasn't going to her. No, it wasn't negotiable.

And he hadn't had the decency to give her any details about it, so of course, if only out of curiosity, she'd decided she had to go. But only after Thad had tracked down the biggest to-go mug he could find so she could bring her daily dose of caffeine with her.

She stalked down the hall, pausing for a moment to take in the caramel marble floors and the artwork on the walls. It was very similar to Ferro's home. Opulent and unrestrained, like no office building she'd been in.

She'd gone for the Zen approach in hers. Bamboo floors, and yes, the little sand gardens on her employees' desks. So she was a little bit of a cliché. She felt it made for a relaxing work atmosphere so it was worth it.

She walked toward the ornate, dark wood reception desk at the end of the walkway, satisfied by the harsh sound her heels made on the floor. It was her favorite part about the makeover she'd gotten a few years back. All the sexy, black shoes. The way her steps sounded on the sidewalk, or on hard floors, made her feel powerful. Confident. Especially after she'd learned to walk in them without falling on her face.

There was a man sitting behind the reception desk, which shocked her. She imagined Ferro would have had some pretty young thing hired to be his assistant. And why not? She did. But no. His assistant was just a very normal-looking, middle-aged man in a blue shirt and tie.

"Hi, I'm here to see Ferro. And yes, he's expecting me."

"Ms. Anderson."

"Yes. That's me. Julia Anderson, Anfalas."

"I am aware," he said, looking back at the computer screen and typing in a few things.

"Are you looking for an appointment? Because I don't think I have one."

"No, I'm sending an email, just a second."

She huffed out a short breath. "I'm just going to go in."

"They're locked."

She didn't turn and look at him again, she just walked on down another corridor, until she got to two, dark wood doors, carved in a similar fashion to the reception desk. "What does he think this is? The Sistine Chapel?" she muttered as she approached the doors and pushed on the door handles. They didn't budge. Stupid Ferro.

She knocked, hard.

"Yes?"

"It's your dream date, Calvaresi, open up."

She heard his heavy footsteps crossing the office, then both doors swung open. "Did Jerry give you a hard time?"

"Is that his name? Yeah, he treated me like the enemy at the gate."

"Well, he must not have seen the news this morning. Or he did and he's afraid you're trying to seduce secrets out of me."

"Me? Seduce secrets out of you?"

"You are very much the Femme Fatale, especially with all the black."

She looked down at her skinny jeans and tight top. "Yeah, all set for corporate espionage. Can I come in?"

He stood to the side and she brushed past him and into his office. It was as opulent and overdone as the rest of the building with marble and wood trim, art pieces and vases. And in here there was even a very plush, very busy oriental rug.

No one could accuse Ferro of minimalism.

She took a seat in one of the leather, wingback chairs in front of his desk. "So what was so important that I had to come across town before I finished my coffee?" She held her mug aloft. "So I could talk to you?"

"Did you see the news?"

"Been busy." She'd been avoiding it. After the explosion that had happened after their first public outing she'd been genuinely terrified of what might be in the paper today. And she really, really didn't want to see pictures of them making out. She really didn't.

"Then let me enlighten you." He smiled and picked up a tablet device from his desk. He touched a news app and it opened, giving headline after headline, from tech blogs, to traditional news publications, about Julia Anderson and Ferro Calvaresi's scorching affair.

Heat pricked her face when she saw the photos. Each article had more than one of them, revealing, sexual. And the look on her face was much too sincere. There she was, pressed against the wall, her arms twined around Ferro's neck, their lips fused together. She had to admit, they made a pretty hot couple. She actually looked okay with him, not completely out of place.

"Well. Wow," she managed after a few minutes.

"And that's not the best part," he said.

"Oh. Yay."

"The talk in the online forums, and on the tech blogs, isn't as negative as it was yesterday. There's some buzz that there may be a big merger coming. They're already speculating about what the love child, so to speak, between Anfalas and Datasphere would look like."

"But there isn't."

"Barrows will be the love child. That navigation system. And we'll have the prebuzz. Can you imagine it? Can you imagine how desirable this product is going to be by the time it hits? This is better than we could have imagined."

It didn't feel better, it felt… It was making her dizzy. "You do know how to spread a rumor, don't you?"

"Not just me. And in the age of media run by the masses things can spread at unbelievable speed. Even if they're half-truths and speculation, people take them as gospel. And once it's out there like this…eradicating it isn't possible. All you can do is skew it to work in your favor."

"You're a master there, aren't you?" She thought of that biography. Of all the secrets it had spilled. She wondered if any of it was true.

It seemed too fantastic to be real, honestly. She didn't see how it could be true. A boy from the streets of Rome, barely scraping by, started making murky connections, dating wealthy women, manipulating them for their money. Then saving, investing, starting up a company and becoming one of the richest, most powerful men in the world.

Yep. Far too unbelievable to be real. And yet, Ferro had never corrected the rumors. He'd never said a thing about them. Had never seemed affected. He'd just smiled, that Calvaresi smile, and shined it on any reporter who asked. No denial, no confirmation.

If anything, the rumors had made him more popular. Women already loved him, and the idea that he'd managed to use his body to earn his success only made him more intriguing. Rare was the computer genius with a body like Ferro's, and he was consistently ranked one of the sexiest people alive. The year the biography had come out, he'd been top of the list.

Oh, no, the rumors had never hurt him. And he'd never seemed at all bothered by any of the talk.

"I'm not a novice," he said. "Anyway, this is all going as we planned. Now all we need to do is get a product proposal into Barrows."

"Oh, that's all."

"We're two of the greatest minds in the world, I'm sure we can come up with something."

"Or kill each other trying," she said.

"That is a possibility."

She bit her lip and debated saying anything else. She totally resented having to ask him this, but, all things considered, it would look really strange if she didn't. She'd almost asked yesterday, but even then she'd been sort of hoping there would be a way around it.

Because the plan was to go back to the way things had always been at the end of this. And the more time she spent with him, the harder it would be. And this…this was going to require a lot of time spent together.

But she was trapped. They were trapped. Hoist by their own petard, as it were.

"I have a…thing," she said. "An event thing. And it was to Julia and Guest and since I was Guest at the *Cold Planet* premiere and the charity, I thought you should maybe be Guest at this."

"I see. And what is it exactly?"

She flinched. "A wedding? It's for one of my staff members and she invited me and this is a huge industry type of event and if we don't go together after all that, then what's even the point?"

She was rambling because she knew that he would probably like to go to a wedding like he wanted a hole in the head, but it only made sense.

"If I go alone people will ask questions," she said, sensing from his silence that he was not amused at the thought of being roped into this.

"And why didn't you ask me yesterday?"

She winced. "I was hoping to come up with an exit strategy. I failed."

"No exit door past this point, *cara mia*."

"Obviously," she said. "Which is why I am now asking you. But I was waiting until I had no other option."

"I see. And when is this wedding?"

"Next weekend."

"Saturday or Sunday?"

She flinched again. "It's kind of an extended thing."

"Why is that?"

"Because it's a destination wedding. Very trendy. Especially for a highly paid junior executive at a very successful tech company."

"And where is the destination?"

"It's sort of in Alaska."

"Who gets married in Alaska?" That's what she'd asked.

"It's a very beautiful resort. And the bride's family is from there, so it's a returning to her roots…thing." That had been the bride's answer anyway.

"And you expect us to go to Alaska for the weekend. As a couple?"

"Well…yes. Come one, Ferro, you know if I go alone it will cause more trouble than if we go together. We've got this great online buzz and by the time Barrows gets the proposal from us they won't even be surprised. They'll be thrilled in fact since, as you mentioned, everyone is champing at the bit to get a glimpse of the unholy spawn our union will produce."

"That's true."

"Name your price," she said. "I could put some money on the dresser every morning."

The words hung in the air, so awkward and not what she'd intended. It wasn't supposed to be all sexual innuendo-y but it was. She blamed those pictures. Well, and the make-out session that had produced them.

She shook her head. "Oh…gross. I'm sorry, that wasn't what I—"

"Don't apologize, *cara mia*." He smiled, and it was so off considering the situation. He hadn't been in full charm mode thirty seconds ago and now he looked… There was something haunted in his eyes and she didn't like it. But it was gone almost as soon as she identified it. "A joke. I get it."

"Great," she said.

"And of course I'll go to the wedding with you. There's no work I can't do remotely so it won't mess with anything on that score."

"Great."

"We will have to share a room, you know that, of course?"

"Maybe they'll just think we're old-fashioned and sleep separately?"

He gave her a hard look. "I doubt it. But won't there be more than one bedroom in the suite?"

She winced. "Well, no. Because all the suites were booked."

"What?"

"I mean, I still have a suite, but it's this big, one room sort of thing. All open."

"And how did that come to pass?"

"I went to book the best room, then felt like a jerk because the bride and groom should have the best room. So I got the Royal Suite for Dana and Josh. But then I thought her parents and his parents needed nice rooms, so I booked the town house suites for the families."

He let out a long breath. "And let me guess, the bridal party needed rooms, too."

"Well. Yes."

"You're generous to your own detriment, *cara*. But in advance, I'll tell you I'll be sleeping on the couch."

Ferro watched the color in Julia's cheeks darken. She was still mortified from her previous gaffe regarding leaving the money on the dresser, he could tell. She was the rare person not quite jaded enough by failure or success. Things still affected her, and in spite of her armor, her emotions were still visible. But he wasn't going to comfort her. It wasn't his job to make her feel all right about herself. He shouldn't feel compelled to tell her it was all right.

She doesn't know about your past.

No, she didn't. But it didn't matter if she did.

A twinge in his chest called that a lie. He did care. He didn't like people thinking he'd manipulated women out of their fortune by seduction. But the truth was worse. The truth that he wasn't the one doing the manipulating.

Still, her little joke was cutting a bit too close to the past. They were trading, not sexual favors, but they were walking a fine line. The kiss had proven that. She had been affected by it, he could tell. He hadn't been. She had been interesting to kiss. Inexpert and clumsy, enthusiastic in a way he'd never experienced before.

But in truth, it had been just like the times in his past. Times when he'd had to do things to survive, whether he wanted to or not. When he'd had to use the only asset he'd possessed to get ahead. To survive.

He'd been smart, but mainly uneducated. A hard worker, but not able to get jobs that would truly advance him.

Then he'd met Claudia. And everything had changed.

You want to make money, caro, *you use what you have.*

Why be hungry when you have something people will buy? A nice body. Women will pay to use you, and you will be rich.

No mention of the cut she'd taken, but in the end, she was right. He had gotten rich. Though, mainly through investing the money he earned.

But in order to do a job like that he'd had to learn how to detach his mind from his body. A perfect division of the two. It was the only way to feel okay. To survive it. Otherwise… otherwise the shame was crippling. So he'd built walls around himself. Now it was like second nature. He flipped it on and off like a switch. He'd been a casual observer to the kiss with Julia and she had clearly been an active participant.

Again, not unusual for him, but it left a bad taste in his mouth.

This was why he avoided relationships. Why he avoided women. Because as skilled as he was at separating mind from body, he couldn't put them back together now. It was all a transaction. All about him giving, then taking payment. It was all he understood, and he was burned out on it.

Twelve years on and it still made his skin feel like it was coated in dirt. Still made him feel like his body belonged to other people. Like he was a product, waiting to be used for the buyer's pleasure. He still felt that his past clients owned little pieces of him. Like he'd been torn apart and parceled off.

But not his mind. They had nothing of his mind. Only his body.

He didn't want to go back to that. Didn't want to spend any time reliving it. Which was why it was better to simply let go of physical pleasure. He didn't know how to handle it all in the right way anyway. It wasn't the same for him.

But Julia was a woman. A normal woman, who was not unaffected by his touch and that meant he had to be careful. He wasn't going to use her body against her. He was determined not to do that, no matter what.

There were depths he would not sink to. He would use her, but only so far as she used him. But in terms of sexual desire they were on two different playing fields, and he would never, ever do to her what had been done to him.

He would never use her body to his own ends. Because he could. It would be so very easy…

"Well, that's a relief. And also, gentlemanly to give me the bed."

"I assume you're paying for the room."

"But you're my date," she said.

"I'm Guest. You're the name on the invitation. And you footing the bill is the only thing giving you a preferential sleeping position, so if you want me to pay…"

"I'm pretty sure I can afford it, Ferro, or did you not see that I'm the richest woman in the world."

"I did, it was an interesting article."

"Well, I can afford a hotel room. And I want the bed."

"I can afford one, too."

"Yeah, yeah, I read your article, too. And hey, you were reading about me?" The expression on her face was funny, a mix of delight and insecurity. Julia was a savvy businesswoman, no question, but there was something beneath it, too. Something that seemed to shine through the armor sometimes. A glimpse at someone young, easily excited and bursting with dreams.

He wondered why she covered that part of herself up in black and leather. Why she tried to pretend she was blasé and unaffected when she was clearly anything but. He wondered why she'd put on her armor in the first place.

"I was reading the article, it turned out you were the star."

"Yeah, I've done all right for myself. We've done all right for ourselves." That made his stomach feel odd.

"We have."

"So, I'm going to go and get back to my desk and my assistant that does not treat me like the dirt on the bottom of his shoes. Will you need me for anything else this week?"

"I shouldn't. We don't need the business proposal in for another two weeks."

"Great, then I'll spend the week getting everything in order for me to be gone for a few days. And I'll uh…see you at the wedding."

She turned and walked out of the office, her strides long and purposeful, the flick of her long blond hair leaving a cloud of lavender behind.

Any normal man would surely be plotting to seduce her over the weekend. He imagined if she had brought another date, she would have been seduced.

Instead she was bringing him. And seduction was not on his agenda. He was far too familiar with it, and it had left a bad taste in his mouth that lingered years after the fact.

This was all about business. And he no longer had to use his body for the sake of business. Now it was just a matter of chipping away at his soul, when the occasion demanded. Lucky for him, he was so accustomed to it that it barely hurt anymore.

No, he'd managed to find ways to block all that out. And now, even when he wanted to feel something, all that remained was a dark, empty void. He had removed his pain, along with everything good.

He looked around his office, at the pristine, glimmering room that was evidence of all he had achieved. The trade, in his estimation, had been worth it.

CHAPTER SIX

IT WAS OFFICIAL, her Alaska outfit was kick-ass. Which was good, because she needed a little of that to get her through dealing with a long weekend of Ferro in a hotel room. *Gulp*.

She tugged at the zipper on her black jacket and put her hands on her hips, black leather pants feeling appropriately tough and awesome against her skin. Then she crossed her arms beneath her breasts and waited on the already-way-too-warm-for-these-clothes tarmac for Ferro to arrive so she could board his private plane.

Clothes really did do something for the way she felt. She'd doubted that when she'd first been thrust into the public arena. Monochromatic had always been her strategy. Black helped her match and blend in. And especially after the assault she'd stopped trying to fit in and just gone with baggy T-shirts with funny sayings and baggy pants with too many zippers.

She didn't wear color. Especially pink. Not after the prom dress.

You'll look so pretty in it, honey.

The image of her standing in front of the mirror at the department store, her mother behind her, beaming, flashed through her mind. They'd spent hours dress shopping after Michael had asked her to be his date.

That same dress had been torn, destroyed by the end of the night. And when she'd taken it off, let it fall to the bathroom floor before stepping into the shower to scrub the blood and pain and shame away, she'd vowed she would never wear that stupid, insipid color again.

At first, her publicist and stylist had tried to push her into softer clothes, but eventually, they'd figured out a style that kept some of her edge while giving her polish.

It was armor. It made her look more like she wanted to feel. Tougher, more in control. Like she had mastered that silly girl looking desperately for acceptance. Like she was tough enough to take on the world. She still felt like a shivery mass of Jell-O inside half the time.

But hey, at least she looked the part, even if she couldn't be the part.

"All ready for snowdrifts, I see."

She turned and watched Ferro stride toward her, with a fully appropriate level of female appreciation for the way the man looked in a pair of dark jeans that rode low on lean hips, a white, button-up shirt with sleeves pushed up to his elbows and a leather bag slung over his shoulder.

"And you're not."

"Well, I thought I might change on the plane. It has more bedrooms than the hotel suite you booked us."

"Aha. Ha, ha. Cute, Calvaresi."

"But it is true."

"Well, I'll find out soon, won't I?" She picked her suitcase up from the ground and looked at him. "Give the order, or, whatever you have to do to get this show on the road. I don't want to linger on the runway. I'm sweltering."

He smiled and pulled his phone out of his jacket pocket.

"You know, there's a faster, better phone than that on the market," she said. "OnePhone. To rule them all."

"Better is a generalization and is also subjective. Also, your phone is only faster when it's able to hook up to your special cell towers which is in…remind me, Julia, ten percent of cases?"

She smiled. "Twelve. But we're expanding."

"Right, right." He pushed a button on his phone and the door to the plane opened, the stairs lowering. "In the meantime, my phone continues to be functional. And it makes calls without dropping them."

"Yeah, super functional. I bet all the people with private planes want your phone. Meanwhile, the masses who want to fling birds at pigs, really like my phone."

"A waste of tech."

"No, it's not." She started climbing the stairs and ducked her head when she entered the plane. "Nice. Bigger than mine," she said, sitting on one of the plush leather sofas. "Anyway, when I was in high school, we were all starting to get phones. And they did one thing, they made calls. Great. The screens were black-and-white, the ring tones were monophonic. Really rich kids got a laptop, too. Now? Now a whole computer is available on your phone. Web browsing, videos and, yes, games. Accessibility. There's a price point, not just for phones, but for all technology for almost everyone now. Information, entertainment. All in your hand."

"I'm going to skip the potential double entendre inherent in comments about handheld entertainment."

She curled her lip. "Please do."

"But I do see your point. You see yourself as a bit of a revolutionary, don't you?"

"I do. We're changing the landscape here, Ferro, changing the way people interact and learn. It's an amazing thing we do here."

"I'm just in it for the money," he said.

"Really?" She studied his expression, tried to get a read on him. "I don't believe that. You have to have a passion for this."

"No, Julia, I don't. I'm good with computers, I picked up

an understanding of them easy, but like every other thing in my life, they were just a way out. I only care about the money. That's why, in the end, I'm your biggest threat, and don't forget it. Hamlin likes power, and one day, soon, I hope, he'll have reached for too much too soon. You are a visionary. Passionate and idealistic, and mark my words, that will be your downfall. All I care about is getting ahead. I don't care about right, or wrong. I only care about winning the game."

There was such a bleak hardness to his statement. Such cold calculation. But she wasn't sure if there was truth to it. She was almost positive he believed it to be true, though she wasn't sure why he needed to.

Finally she spoke. "What happens at the end? What happens when you're done and there's nothing left to do?"

"I find a new game." No emotion in his tone, no fire.

"I'll take passion and the potential to lose then," she said. "I think it's more fun."

"I haven't had the luxury of having fun in my life."

"You're a billionaire, Ferro, several times over. Relax and enjoy it."

He shook his head and the engine on the plane kicked into gear, the roaring in her ears as it started to move down the runway. "That's something you learn early on when you live on the street, *cara*. Never get comfortable. Never take it for granted. You never sleep. Not really. You have to be ready to jump up and fight for your life at any given moment. Complacency will be the death of you, and I believe it's true in business, as well."

Julia's throat tightened. "And now…now that you have your mansion with all your security…do you sleep now?"

He shook his head slowly, his eyes focused on a point past her. "No."

"Then you might as well be back on the street."

He laughed. "I fight every day to make sure I never go back."

"Your life sounds exhausting."

"This from the woman with boundless energy?"

She shrugged. "I'm happy, though. It's easier to live when you're happy."

"Why are you happy?"

"I have my dream job. Friends. Family." She nearly stumbled over that word. She hardly ever spoke to her parents. Could hardly speak to her mother at all. "Why wouldn't I be happy?"

"Why so much armor, then? If you're so happy, why are you so well-protected?"

"I don't know what you're talking about."

He leaned forward, extending his hand and sliding his thumb and forefinger over the collar of her jacket. "You know full well what I'm talking about. I'm talking about this."

"Are your suits armor, Ferro? Or are they just something you wear to create an image."

"Armor," he said. "So that no one can say I look like the street urchin that I am. So that, no matter the rumors, I look like a man who earned my success, rather than a man who slept his way to the top. Underneath, though, it doesn't change a damn thing, that's the rub."

"It does. I would feel a lot worse about myself if I had to go up on stage for presentations with my limp hair, braces and baggy shirts."

"But it doesn't change you. Not really. If it did, even if you were in baggy T-shirts you would feel confident."

"Such an expert for a man who is so freaking dysfunctional."

"But I'm right. You know I am."

"So? Everyone does it. You do it, you just said."

He nodded. "I suppose they do. Image, as they say, is everything. Unlike you, though, I don't pretend that I'm all right."

She didn't like that assessment. Didn't like that he seemed to think she was pretending to be fine. Or that it felt true. In that moment, she felt very much like the girl she'd been in high school, like a little kid playing dress up.

"Well, when you're comfortable throwing off your image, I'll ditch mine," she said.

"I'm not challenging you. I'm not even judging you. I'm the last person in a position to pass judgment, and I think we both know that. I'm simply stating a fact. You hide a lot, Julia. I can feel it."

She didn't like it at all. Didn't like that he knew just what her butt-kicking outfit was for. It made it feel less effective. And he was right, the change wasn't any deeper than her skin, because if it was, he wouldn't have been able to shake her confidence half so quickly.

Jerk.

"Well, next time I'm in the mood for a psychoanalysis I'll hire a professional, okay? I don't need my head read by a guy who has more issues than I do."

She leaned back in her seat, crossed her arms and legs, wiggling her foot in an effort to keep from leaping up and pacing the length of the plane.

"Anyway," she said. "How happy are you?"

"I never said I was happy." He slid his hand over his chin. "I'm not sure I even know what happiness is. But I am winning the game, and to me that's all that counts."

"This is incredible." Julia shoved her hands in her pockets and blew out a breath that clouded in front of her face and hung in the crisp, cold air for a moment before fading away on the wind.

The hotel was set on the edge of a lake, surrounded by

mountains and tall evergreen trees that secluded them in a wall of green and blues.

Ferro looked around, his expression impassive.

"You don't seem thrilled," she said, pulling a scarf out of her bag and wrapping it around her neck.

"I don't like the cold," he said simply, walking toward the entrance of the hotel.

It was made from rough hewn logs, polished and stained the color of honey. A luxury cabin set out in the wilderness. She'd been completely taken with the city when she'd moved out West to California. With the heat and palm trees. With the sheer difference between Cali and her hometown. But this was something else entirely, more incredible in some ways. Because all people could hope to do was come out here and survive. No matter how beautiful the hotel was, it seemed pulled into the landscape. As if the wild had claimed it, rather than humans claiming any sort of civilization.

"Then we'll go inside," she said, following him through the glass doors that slid open and admitted them into the lobby. "Nice," she said, looking around at the sleek, wood interior. "Big fish statue." She pointed to the iron representation of a sockeye salmon. "That's pretty cool. And hey, it's for sale. I could buy it and stick it in my house." She was rambling and she wasn't sure why. Maybe because she was getting used to wicked Ferro and stoic Ferro was throwing her off a little bit.

"I would like to see that, Julia," he said. "A salmon in your beachfront mansion."

"Hey, it's…sort of to theme."

"And sort of not."

She smiled and tried to draw a smile out of him. She managed, but there was something terribly false about it. And she didn't know if it was because this one was false, where all the others had been real. Or if she was just seeing something different in his expression after their conversation on the plane. After his assertion that he didn't know what happiness was.

This was exactly what she was afraid of. That more time with Ferro would make him human. Would make her get him. Might make her care.

No way. Ferro was a jerk. She could not, would not, care about him.

"Just a second and I'll check in," she said.

Ferro looked around the lobby and waited for the sophisticated heating system to take effect. He didn't know why he'd let the temperature bother him. It wasn't like he hadn't experienced cold in the past few years, but truth be told, he did go out of his way to avoid it.

And ever since they'd gotten off the plane he'd been battling with the thought of what it would have been like to be stuck outside here. To have to suffer through a night dealing with the elements.

The fact that he'd moved to a place with a temperate climate wasn't by chance. He liked to be warm. Didn't like to remember what it was like to sleep on cold cement or dirt, covered in cardboard.

It was the same reason he didn't like to be hungry. The same reason he didn't deal with relationships.

He didn't like reminders. Reminders of how worn down he'd been when Claudia had found him. She'd seen him standing on the street, asking for work. And she'd offered.

Do you want a bed to sleep in tonight, sweetheart?

He still remembered her first words to him. The way her perfume smelled. How his skin had smelled after, her perfume clinging to him along with his shame. She had paid a lot of money for his virginity. She'd found it exciting to train him. And it had provided him with a week's worth of food and a small hotel room. One night of sex, a week of comfort.

And when his money was spent, Claudia found him again.

I need you again, sweetheart. And when I'm done with you...I have friends, you know? Lonely. Neglected by their husbands. I'm sure they'd love a chance to get to play with you. If you say yes, forget staying in a little hotel. You can buy your own place. How does that sound? Independence? Heat?

Impossible to turn down. But every dollar earned cost so damn much.

"All checked in!"

He looked at Julia, at her figure, the way her clothes, even her down-lined trench coat, conformed to her body. She would be warm. He didn't doubt that. Her skin was soft, he knew that already. And she would be warm.

He flexed his fingers, curled his hand into a fist, trying to get the phantom impression of her flesh off him.

A strange sort of heat fired its way through him. Just the thought of her warmed him when, a moment before, he'd been freezing from the inside out. Interesting. But not something he was going to pay attention to.

He followed her, wordlessly, to the elevator and let her push the buttons, taking them up to a high floor. A room with a view, no doubt.

The doors opened and he followed Julia down the hall, her shoes clicking on the wood floor. She liked to take long, hard steps. He'd noticed that about her early on. All a part of her armor. To seem tough. To seem impenetrable.

"It's on the end," she said, chipper, sliding her keycard into the reader and pushing the door open.

The room was, as she'd said, completely open with massive floor-to-ceiling windows offering views of the lake and mountains. There was a couch, and one large bed, framed in wooden poles that looked hand-carved.

Most men would be thinking about all the activity that could be accomplished in a bed that size. He, in fact, started to.

Do as you're told, boy. You're not here for you. You're here for me. For my pleasure. I own you.

That was the real Claudia. Not the woman who acted like she wanted to help a young man with no place to sleep. The woman who took pleasure in owning him. In selling him. That voice was always in the back of his mind, reminding him just how dirty he was.

No matter how much he tried to convince himself that none of it mattered, it did. It did.

Because there was no freedom from it. There was no escaping the fear of being cold, no matter how many years you'd spent warm since. There was no escaping the feeling that your body belonged to someone else. No matter how long it had been since you sold it.

The fact remained, he had sold it. And somehow, he had never felt that he'd gotten it back.

"Nice," she said, "and, only the one bed, as advertised." Her cheeks turned pink and he wondered if it was all down to embarrassment, or if she desired him?

If she desired him, the entire game they were playing would be easier. So much easier if one of them was feeling something genuine.

And he would know how to use that desire. To make it burn hotter for him. Brighter. He was trained, after all, to give a woman exactly what she wanted.

He rebelled at the idea, though. He had already played with her once, at the charity event he had used her emotion to bring on arousal, had used his expertise against her, to make her enjoy the kiss even though she loathed him.

He knew for a fact that with the right thoughts in mind, it was possible to be turned on even when you hated everything happening to your body. That it was possible to find a place deep enough that you controlled everything with your mind.

He gritted his teeth.

"Yes, but I am still willing to take the couch, no argument."

"Great."

"Will there be media at this wedding?"

"Yes, lots. That's why I knew we needed to go together. Josh is a Colter, you know, of The Colters who own the restaurant chain, so it's a big deal."

"And still you booked everyone's rooms? They must all be millionaires at minimum."

"My wedding gift," she said.

He looked at her, trying to read her, trying to figure her out. She was insecure, yes, he'd read that early on. Compliments would go a long way with her, because she was hungry for external validation. And yet, also, she did these things that were just nice.

She gave to people for no reason and he found he had a hard time understanding that.

Or maybe it wasn't so much niceness. Maybe she was buying friends. Yes, that made sense to him. Especially knowing what he did about her.

"And your attempt at buying friends?" he asked.

She frowned. "Everyone does nice things for their friends."

"I don't."

"Do you have friends?"

"I don't think so."

"Why not?"

"Because. At this point in life, yes, I would always feel I was buying them. I'm not particularly likable, in case you hadn't noticed."

"No, I had."

"I came to the world stage with nothing. There are no connections from my past I wish to maintain."

She sighed. "I'm not buying friends. I'm doing this because I want to, and I can, so why not? I do find that problem with dates, though," she said, sitting on the edge of the bed.

"Do you?"

"Yes. Gold diggers. I am a meal ticket to almost every man that wants to go out with me and it's really, really tiring. The big question I ask myself before I agree to go out with a guy is would he have dated me before I had money? If the answer is no, I don't bother anymore."

"And how do you gauge that?"

"Men of a certain…handsomeness threshold," she said, "are not with me because of my brains."

"Stereotyping."

"But I've found it to be true. I had a uh…incident in high school."

"More of your past hardship?"

The cynicism in his voice had her turning away from the urge to share. "What about you? You don't have friends, but I've seen the sort of women you take to events."

Yes, he was very selective about the kind of woman he took to parties. Beautiful, shallow. He bought their dresses, their jewelry, he let them hang on his arm and have his picture taken. And at the end of the night, they always went their separate ways.

He had never started out intending it to be that way, but the voice was always there. Interrupting desire. Destroying his lust.

"I don't care what they're after," he said. "As long as we both get what we want."

He got to present the image he wanted to give to the press, they got diamonds, exposure, the thrill of being with a celebrity, whatever it was that got them off. So long as it wasn't sex.

"Gee, you're like most of my dates."

"No, I don't use. I trade. And anyway, you think it's better to try to guess what they want before you get in too deep?"

"Okay, so that sucks. But so does finding out the guy who you've gone on four dinner dates with is a gay man in a committed relationship trying to get close to you to get to your money. By the way, the man he was in the relationship with had no idea, and he was very, very unhappy to discover us together at the trendy restaurant I had taken him to."

"At least he only took advantage of your wallet and not your body."

"I know," she said, biting her lip. "I really do. But it would be nice to go out with someone who clearly just didn't want to use you. Back before…before Anfalas, everyone in my life always made it very clear that there was something wrong with me. And now, yeah, now I'm popular because I dress well and I have money."

She looked away from him then, out the window. He felt something strange happen to his chest. Like there was an invisible thread that ran between them and he could feel what she did. Or maybe it was just what she'd said. The desire to feel what normal people did, if only for a moment. He didn't usually worry about it, but sometimes he wondered. What it might be like if his body, heart and brain worked together instead of as separate entities.

Wondered what it would be like if he could scrub the dirt from his skin and walk on. Clean. Like nothing had happened.

But it wasn't possible.

He shrugged. "That's the way the world works, Julia. The man with the money holds the power, or in your case, the woman with the money. Do you think anyone gave a damn about me when I was a poor orphan? When I was living on the streets?"

She shook her head. "I'm sure they didn't otherwise…you wouldn't have been on the street, would you?"

"No one cared when my mother died," he said. "Because she had nothing to give anyone. She only had a son, a son no one wanted to look after. A boy who fell through the cracks."

"How did you survive?" she asked.

"For a while? The church. I lived there for a few years, went to the school the nuns ran. But after a while there wasn't enough money to care for me, and I found myself homeless again."

"I suppose that makes my complaints about gold-digging men sound a little silly."

She looked away, her expression sad. He should compliment her. She'd just fed him the best information, told him that she craved that sort of male attention. She was giving him ample material to use against her. A chance to form a bond that he could use to his advantage later. After he took down Hamlin. When it was time to take Anfalas, and Julia, out, too. He could use this in conjunction with information already in place. All he had to do was use it.

But he didn't. And he wasn't sure why.

Perhaps because she was honest. Her words weren't designed to manipulate. She was truly giving something of herself, and no one had ever done that with him before. No one had ever made him want to share his past before. Just now, he'd told her more than he'd ever told anyone else before.

Again, he felt that strange sort of warmth. Fire licking at his veins.

"Are you hungry?" he asked.

She turned to face him. "Uh…sure?"

"Good. Let's go find something for dinner."

"O-okay. Just let me get something on other than this."

He nodded, and suddenly, he was assaulted by an image of her peeling those leather pants from her body. The flames burned hotter.

"I'll meet you in the lobby."

He strode out of the hotel room and closed the door behind him. And he was cold again.

CHAPTER SEVEN

JULIA TRIED TO shake the little shiver that seemed to cling to her skin whenever Ferro was around. It would be so convenient to blame the Alaskan chill, but it wasn't really fair or accurate since she'd felt this way ever since their kiss on the balcony.

She wrapped her shawl more tightly around her shoulders. Red, which was unusual for her, paired with matching shoes and lipstick, and a fitted black dress, all provided by her stylist with explicit instructions. Along with every other outfit she would wear this weekend.

True horror had been discovering that her very helpful assistant, who did not know her affair with Ferro was fake because she couldn't have anyone privy to that, had ensured that a different horrifically see-through negligee was provided for every night.

This had prompted her to send Thad a very angry text message about her being in the frozen tundra. His response had been that skin-to-skin contact was the best way to reduce hypothermia. He suggested she get that "delicious bastard" naked and snuggle up for safety.

Her follow-up text had been unrepeatable in polite society.

Ferro was waiting for her at the bar in the hotel restaurant, a glass of whiskey in hand.

"That ought to warm you up," she said.

His dark brows shot up. "Who said I needed to be warmed up?"

"Earlier you said you didn't like to be cold."

His lips curved into a half smile. "I guess I did." He knocked back the rest of the whiskey, his face remaining placid when she knew his throat had to burn. "Let's get a table."

"Sure."

Ferro flagged down the hostess and she led them across the restaurant, decked out in the same rustic sophistication as the rest of the hotel. They were seated in a corner at a table fashioned from a ring of log and polished so that it was smooth.

"I really like it here," she said when they were seated. "It all kind of reminds me of something from a fantasy movie. I can imagine dwarves eating here. Though, it would need to be more rustic and less polished. But the idea, I mean."

If biting her tongue would take the stupid, revealing statement back, then she would do it. What was it about Ferro that brought her inner geek out in full force? Maybe it was just that she wasn't used to spending so much time with someone who wasn't a part of her inner circle. She didn't have to play around with Thad, he knew her, he kept her on track. Her stylist, Sophie, had seen her at her worst in terms of wardrobe and she didn't seem to care at all.

And her employees, well, most of them were as out of the mainstream as she was. But with Ferro, before this, she'd tried to maintain her image. Because he was one of the enemies, and she never wanted him to see a hole in her armor. Had never wanted him to catch a glimpse of just how human she was.

And that came from the fact that Ferro himself seemed inhuman.

He was a wall of unreadable emotion. Pure granite.

Soft little things like herself were easily squished by something as immobile as rock, and she should remember that. And not think about their kiss. Or the shiver that went over her skin whenever she looked into those dark, fathomless eyes.

But then he surprised her. "Perhaps you should use it as an inspiration for a game setting. For your phone. We could coordinate and make one that runs on my phone's platform, as well."

"Oh, that would be fun. Could be one where you build your fantasy world and try to create bigger cities."

"And you can create armies."

"Or live peacefully and hunt and gather," she said, picking her menu up.

"I think it would be a good idea."

"See? Passion. It helps."

"Personally I prefer control. Then things aren't as random. They're much more predictable. Much more orderly."

"Oh, but Ferro, you never reach the heights."

Something in his eyes changed, darkened, his gaze lowering to her lips. She could feel them tingle, just from him looking at them. Well, her lips and parts lower, and she didn't even want to think about that. About how he'd managed such a feat.

With just a look.

"I'm going to get the salmon," she said, doing her best to defuse the tension that seemed to only be felt on her end. "Though I feel a little disloyal to my iron friend in the lobby."

"You have a ruthless streak in you, Julia," he said, his voice husky. "I'll have what you're having."

He put his menu down and leaned back in his chair, his dark eyes never leaving hers. She felt like she was being hunted. A strange, and oddly exhilarating feeling.

"It goes with the passion. Even when it's against my better judgment…I make decisions that are led by emotion. Clearly, or I wouldn't be here. My desire to cut Hamlin out of the picture, to advance my company, my baby, well, that trumps common sense. That's the catch to passion."

"Oh, there's far more than one catch to passion."

"Is there?"

"Yes, passion is extremely selfish. It's personal. And when fueled, it only becomes hungrier. It demands satisfaction no matter the cost."

Her eyes were drawn to his lips now. To the way he spoke the words. The way they moved. She knew how expert they were. How adeptly they could awaken her body.

Passion, just like he was saying, only grew hungrier the more it was fed. Apparently that was true of physical passion, too.

She had limited to no experience with that.

Another thing she kept quiet. Another thing she didn't advertise because, OMG as if she wasn't enough of a geek, she was also still a virgin. At twenty-five. Her only experience had been violent, painful. She was so thankful it had stopped before he'd managed to rape her, because she knew that had been his intent. But even so, it had crippled her confidence with the opposite sex, no matter how much she liked to pretend it didn't.

Maybe that was why she said yes to dates with guys who only wanted her money. Because they were nonthreatening. Because they wouldn't want her.

Even without having a lot of experience with passion, passion that went beyond sci-fi and fantasy films, she could feel the truth of his words. Oh, boy, could she feel them. The shivery feeling was back with a vengeance.

"Is that…I mean, is that so bad when both parties involved are…passionate about the same thing?" She cleared her throat and stumbled on. "You and…and me for example. With the business stuff, I mean. So, I'm very passionate about the Barrows deal and you're…well, you want it, and while we both want it for how it benefits us, in the end, my passion will benefit you and vice versa."

"That's nice when it happens, but in my life, what I have seen is that the one with the most power ends up taking control of the game. And you don't want to be the one out of control."

"So, summation, in Ferro world, control trumps passion."

"Every time, *cara.*"

"But control doesn't help you think of cool games. Check and mate."

He laughed, a sound that seemed pulled from him, as though he wasn't used to it. But she'd heard him laugh a few times. She didn't know why this one seemed different. More genuine.

"I cannot argue with your logic. On that point."

"Great."

Their salmon appeared a few minutes later, with wine, which Julia was very happy to see, all things considered.

They ate in silence for a while, both of them enjoying the view of the lake, which was still brilliant and bright despite the late hour, thanks to the Alaskan summer.

She flashed back to her presentation, nearly two weeks ago now. And she laughed.

"What?" he asked, looking up from his dinner.

"Well," she said, straightening, "two weeks ago you crashed my presentation and I wanted to kill you, cheerfully, with whatever object was readily available. And now, here we are, sitting across from each other, and I have a knife to my right and I don't even want to use it on you."

"We have come a long way."

"Indeed." She took a bite of her rice pilaf. "You almost seem civilized."

"Don't make that mistake, Julia," he said.

"Why? You don't want to have to live up to my expectations?"

"I don't want you to have expectations that are impossible to have met. Don't forget, when this is over, all bets are off. And this experience, you and me, it's not off-the-record. I'm going to remember everything you say to me. Every weakness you show. Every secret you betray. And I will use it against you."

"You've been nothing but honest with me, Ferro. For your sins, you aren't a liar. So I believe you," she said, her throat tightening, aching. Strange. "No worries."

Maybe because he was so determined to not have a moment of connection with her. Maybe because she was starting to feel a connection, however strange, with him.

Something about him certainly touched her, reached deep in her and made her feel things—want things—that she hadn't really given a lot of thought to wanting in a long time.

What? More kissing? More than kissing? With him? That would be really stupid.

Also, though, really delicious.

Wow, she needed help. Professional grade help.

"Are you ready to go?" he asked.

She nodded. Except if they left, they were going to be back in the hotel room. Alone. Together.

"Maybe," she said, "maybe we could go…hike?"

"At nine o clock?"

"It's light out."

"Bears?"

"Oh. Right. Well, I don't really want to run into any bears."

"I didn't think you would."

She sucked in a breath. "Okay. The room then."

Ferro put some bills down on the table. "Since you're paying for our accommodations."

"Noble of you," she said, her stomach tightening. Why was

she reacting like this? It was pathetic. She was strung so tight it was unbelievable. "Oh!" She remembered her pajama situation and nearly panicked. "Um, I will meet you at the room."

"Okay." He shrugged and turned to go, leaving her there.

She breathed out a long, slow gust of air then headed in the direction of the gift shop. She would get sweats. And then she wouldn't feel quite so out of place and thrown off with Ferro staying in her room. Maybe. Probably not. But it was worth a shot.

Ferro reclined on the couch, his eyes on the sky, still illuminated at eleven. Julia had disappeared to take a shower a half hour before, and he was simply lying there, thinking far too much.

Not so much about her naked body beneath the hot spray of water, but of why he shouldn't think of it.

He was allowing the shame to do its job, to be the reminder he needed for why he wouldn't allow himself to give in to feeling attraction for her.

He wasn't just stopping himself from acting, he was stopping himself from wanting.

It was something he was quite accomplished at. He'd learned, early on, to master his body by thinking the right things. Dwelling on the right things. To become aroused when it was needed, to shut it down when it kept him safe.

The bathroom door opened and light spilled into the room in a thin line, that widened until he saw Julia. She was wearing sweats. Gray and baggy and low on her hips, and a black T-shirt with writing on it.

Her hair was captured in a towel on her head.

He tried to remember if he'd ever seen a woman dressed so casually. He had never had a lover. Not a real lover. He'd had clients. Women who paid to be with him. Who paid for him to be their fantasy. And they had their vanity. For him, they were always overly made up, in stiff corsets attempting to defy gravity and nature. As if he had cared. As if there was any way to make the act, or them, more palatable.

Again, he was struck by Julia's softness. Softness she tried so hard to hide. But it was there, even though it was buried deep. And it fascinated him.

She unwound the towel and threw it back into the bathroom, shaking out her wet hair. It hung, stringy and wavy down her back. She walked to the bed and jumped into the middle of it, pulling her tablet computer from her bag and firing it up, illuminating her face with the bright screen.

She stuck headphones in her ears and started tapping at the screen furiously. Playing a game, he figured, especially when a tiny grunt of frustration escaped her lips.

He couldn't help but smile. That passion she was such an advocate for. It was quite something to witness. Beautiful.

She was beautiful. He realized it with a jolt, realized that he wasn't simply observing her beauty as though she were a sunset. But that he felt her beauty. That he wanted to touch it. Possess it.

It was such a strange, sharp ache. A longing that went deep. Something he was sure he must have felt before, but it seemed lost. In a different part of his life. Maybe in a different man. A different man than he'd become.

"What are you playing?"

She startled, her head popping up, her eyes wide. She pulled her headphones off.

"I thought you were asleep," she said, hand on her chest.

"No. Sorry."

"So you were just…skulking. In the shadows."

"I'm lying on the couch, I'm hardly skulking."

"Lurker."

He laughed. Strange how she made him laugh. Normally he chose to laugh, just like he chose to smile. It wasn't involuntary. It wasn't spontaneous or heartfelt. But she actually pulled something from him. A reaction.

One he couldn't control, which made him slightly concerned. Resentful, even. That this woman, who was so much a girl in many ways, had this power over him. And yet, something in him also wanted to tempt it. To take it to the edge and see what happened. It was tempting. So very tempting.

How long since anything had excited him? Since anything had made him feel heat beneath his skin.

He was tired of being cold.

And that was his very sad reality. That no matter how warm and opulent his surroundings, he never warmed up inside.

"Guilty," he said. "I was just admiring your choice of attire."

"You won't even believe what Thad packed for me."

"Your assistant?"

"Yes. He had, well, he had sexy times on his mind so he packed me some…uh…well, not my sweats. But the gift shop accommodated me."

"I like the sweats," he said.

Lace, silk, would not have been as compelling. Because right now, Julia was a woman as he had never seen one. Clean, bare in so many ways. Her armor reduced to nothing.

How easy it would be now, to say the right words. To go from the couch to her bed. A kiss that would turn into two kisses. Which would turn into more. He could touch her softness, feed on her heat.

A shudder went through his body. He *wanted* it. Wanted her. Wanted her body.

The realization of what he was planning, of what he was allowing himself to want, stopped him cold.

Someday, yes, he would take a lover. He had left it far too

long. But it wouldn't be this woman. Not now. He would not under these circumstances.

He could see it in his head.

Your body in exchange for your company. I let Anfalas live without ever tasting interference from me. All I need in return is you. At my command. For my pleasure.

He could do that. Stop all the digging he'd been doing in her company, stop looking for weaknesses to exploit. Offer her payment. And claim her body as his reward.

And he would have become the very thing he hated.

Trading favors. Taking advantage.

No. He would not allow it. He would not give himself the pleasure. Would not put himself through the hell.

He had very little soul left. It cost to get where he was. And what remained was scarred beyond repair. But he would not surrender the rest.

His body throbbed with heat, tormented him with a taste of what could be.

No. Passion was the road to destruction. It was only through control that he would ever find satisfaction. That he would ever be able to find some sort of answer, some sort of peace, for the torment inside him.

CHAPTER EIGHT

JULIA WOKE UP groggy and twitchy. Room sharing with Ferro was proving to be extremely problematic. First off, the man slept in his underwear. Which she hadn't noticed when he'd gone to sleep on the couch, he'd laid down before she had, and had been covered with a blanket.

But then, he'd gotten up before her and the sound of him getting out of bed had woken her up, and she'd opened her eyes just in time to see him, his bare, muscular back and his butt, oh, dear heaven, his butt, in nothing but a pair of stretchy black briefs that hugged the contours of his body in such a way that there were no longer very many secrets between them, disappearing into the bathroom.

Then he'd exited the restroom, not dressed, and giving her a clear outline of the rest of his…secrets, in addition to sculpted abs and chest, dusted with just the perfect amount of dark hair.

He was like a walking female fantasy, conjured from her most base desires. A real man, with hair and muscles and all the good things that came with a healthy dose of testosterone.

She'd never craved those things before, not at a real visceral level, not like the sight of him made her crave them.

Because she didn't let herself. She hated to admit it. She liked to pretend that Michael, that the assault, didn't matter in a sexual context. Because in her head she knew sex wasn't like that. She knew that most men wouldn't hurt her like that. She knew it.

But a part of her didn't truly believe it. And avoiding sex, and men who wanted it, was so much easier than dissecting how she felt.

So, since guys were hardly beating down her bedroom door, it had been easy to let it go and simply fantasize in private when any needs arose. It was safe that way. She didn't have to depend on anyone. She didn't have to trust anyone.

That was the big one.

But Ferro was making her wonder if it was worth the risk to have contact with a body like that. He wouldn't hurt her, or force her. She knew that much.

And hey, maybe he liked her, too. He had kissed her, after all, and he had to have felt something.

Not that she *liked him* liked him. She just thought he was hot. Totally different from *liking* him. She wasn't a dumb girl with a crush. She was a woman. With needs. She wanted to ravish him, not date him.

She pushed her chicken breast across her plate with her fork. It was time for lunch and the wedding was starting in just a couple of hours. And rather than thinking of her employee on her special day, all she could think about was Ferro's muscles. Pathetic. Completely pathetic.

She didn't even like the man. Except she was almost starting to.

But she didn't really know him. She knew that. She really did. And yet, she couldn't seem to remember when she was with him. When she was with him, she bought into the smiles. The laughter.

She was seriously pathetic.

Ferro had skipped the lunch, citing work related issues, and that was just fine with her, because she needed the break.

A Ferro break. Wow, she remembered the days, sweet,

recent days, when a Ferro break was just needed because she couldn't deal with his pranks and smugness and general jerkishness.

Now she needed a Ferro break so her neglected hormones could calm down and stop panting after him for attention. Not happening. Nope.

Because if she gave in to this weird, crazy desire for him it would ruin...it would ruin...nothing. Absolutely nothing. She didn't like him. He didn't like her. They were rivals bent on taking each other down and right now they were on nothing more than a temporary break from trying to obliterate each other professionally.

So sleeping with him would destroy absolutely nothing. They had no chance at a relationship anyway. She didn't even want one with him.

Her realization almost made her dizzy.

Except, she wasn't really the sort of woman who would sleep with a guy she knew she wasn't going to end up with. Was she?

But she also couldn't see ever trusting someone enough to have an actual relationship. And she knew she didn't want to be used for her money, and guys that were just after her for what she could buy them? Those guys were easy to deny. They were ineffective and basically sexless in her eyes.

But Ferro? Ferro didn't want her money. If he wanted to sleep with her then he would at the very least really want her and not just her status.

Heck, her status meant nothing to him. And anyway, they were already using each other to get a business deal, sans sex, so the using would be physical using, which, as long as she went into it eyes wide-open...

Her mother would be so disappointed in her.

She bit her lip. She'd been taught to treat her body, sex, like it was special.

But her mother had paid for the date who had tried to take her virginity from her. Who had ruined, yeah, she would admit it, the way she saw sex for a really long time. So what did it matter? Her mother had never known what was best for her.

All that aside, what did she have to lose? She was hardly wife and mother material anyway. Maybe, for her, a steamy affair would be the best she could do.

An affair with her enemy.

Now why did that excite her more than it repelled her?

She looked up when a man sat down at her table. Blond, handsome. Not handsome in the same devastating way as Ferro, but not unpleasant, either. Maybe that was the answer. Another man. A more sensible man. And they were in public, safe. Maybe he would be a more sensible choice. A man who could answer this sensual need she seemed to be developing but who wasn't quite as full-on as Ferro.

And, you know, not someone she classified as an enemy.

"Hi," she said, smiling, tilting her head to the side and trying to look flirtatious. She'd seen other women do it, she thought she should be able to pull it off. Plus, her boobs looked really good in the dress she was wearing which, really should help capture attention.

"Hi. Julia Anderson, right?"

"Yes," she said. She didn't feel breathless, but she tried to sound it because she was pretty sure men liked that. "And you are?"

"David Brown. I saw you sitting here and just had to come over."

She lifted her shoulder and pushed her arm in, drawing a little attention to her assets. "Really? That's so nice."

"I have a product idea that I have to pitch to you."

After that, her brain just sort of shut down while David, who was looking less and less handsome, started pitching some half-thought-out idea that didn't have any basis in current technology, or clearly any understanding of how computers worked. Or any idea that walking up to a woman at a wedding and making a business presentation to her was an automatic no.

She was pretty sure when he finished, she shook his hand and thanked him, smiling and pretending like she wasn't dying inside.

She was so sick of it. Of the fact that when she was no one, no men talked to her. Because she was gangly and liked computers more than she liked going out. And that now she had money and status good-looking men approached her frequently. That people were nice. That they treated her with deference because she had power.

That they were all liars. That she couldn't trust anything they said, anything they did. Ferro was a bastard, but he was honest. He wasn't the kind of guy to act charming until he got you alone.

And there was actually a lot to be said about that.

She looked around the room, around the amazing setting. Would she have been friends with this couple if not for her status? If she didn't buy people the best rooms in the hotel, would they still want her around?

One thing was certain. If she couldn't throw money at them, she would have to give something of herself. Open herself up to them. And she didn't like that idea at all.

Ferro didn't like her much, he didn't pretend to. He didn't want to know her, but he might just want to sleep with her. And she could handle that. At least it was clear-cut. At least it was honest.

Right now she would rather have his brutal honesty than a smile from a sycophant.

An affair with her enemy was sounding less and less stupid.

* * *

"You aren't supposed to wear black to weddings."

Ferro approached Julia at the reception, a glass of champagne in hand. He'd come in just as the ceremony was starting, after doing some business with China.

Julia turned and his stomach tightened, blood rushing hot and fast through his veins. And he felt it, strong and sure, arousal.

"I have permission," she said, smiling, her teeth a flash of white against the crimson of her lipstick.

Her blond hair was styled in soft waves, the black dress a simple silhouette that clung tight to her hips and flared out like a bell at her knees, falling softly to the ground from there. But it was the neckline, a plunging V in the front and back, that had his attention.

Her breasts were small, but perfectly formed. And he found himself wondering about them to the point of obsession. Was it due to so many years when his own fantasies had to stay locked inside of himself while he catered to others? So many years spent suppressing desire so he didn't have to deal with past memories? Was that why it was so strong? Or was it simply Julia?

Forbidden fruit. A temptation he never thought he would be vulnerable to.

Because he had been that for other people and there was no satisfaction there for the object of that kind of lust. It was a selfish desire. It used the other party, until there was nothing left of them. Until they were cold inside.

Unless he made it his mission to satisfy her.

No.

He would not do it. He was stained by his past, every penny he'd ever spent, every penny multiplied, coming from his deepest shame. His entire empire had been built on his back, in a near literal sense. He wouldn't bring it all back. He wouldn't.

He hated the rumors. That he had seduced wealthy older women out of their fortunes. But he hated the truth more. That he had been their toy. That he had been bought. That his company was built that way. That his legacy was that of a man who had sold cheaply what should only be given.

So he looked away from her figure. Looked at her eyes. Blue. Clear. Reflecting everything he was starting to think she was: innocence. Goodness. All that armor to cover the sweet and vulnerable that was in her.

"Special permission for the wedding's benefactor?" he asked, handing her the flute of champagne.

She took it, lifted it to her lips, then lowered it. "I'm hardly the benefactor," she said.

"You paid for everyone's accommodations. And you also pay the bride's salary."

"I don't give her money for nothing. She's a darn fine programmer."

"Do you know all of your employees?"

She shrugged one bare shoulder. "Not all of them. At a company the size of mine, that's impossible, but then, you know that."

"I barely know one of mine. Not below a certain tier," he said.

"How is that possible?"

"I'm not the kind of boss who does walk-throughs of the office and team meetings and wilderness camping trips where we do trust exercises."

"Oh. I am. I mean, I've done those things," she said.

"Yes, you are a very...you are a nice person."

"Thank you," she said. "You say that like you're surprised."

"I don't know very many nice people."

"Maybe I'm not that nice, Ferro."

"Why do you say that?"

"I don't know. I mean, I guess I'm generous. With money. But not with me. Yeah, I walk through the halls of the office building and I tell everyone good game. I come to their wedding and I buy expensive gifts. But money is so easy to give. It's a lot harder to give you. To give real friendship."

"You want people to use you for your money," he said, the words slipping out.

"I never thought of it that way, but I suppose it's what I earn, since it's all I give. Still, human nature being the fickle, hypocritical thing it is, I've never cared for being used for my money when I was…trying to make a connection."

"And men do that to you?"

"Yeah. There are a lot of beautiful women in the world, Ferro, much more beautiful than I am. But there are no women with more money than me. So…doesn't take a genius to figure out why guys are attracted to me, suddenly."

"Any man who looks at you and only sees a bank balance is an idiot. How could anyone miss how truly amazing and unique you are?"

Her eyes rounded, his compliment hitting its mark. Except, it had been genuine. He wasn't trying to seduce. Wasn't trying to play. Still the words had come out and he knew they had worked. They were drawing her in.

If you want her, you can have her.

No. He wouldn't.

Still, the temptation burned so hot he was nearly consumed with it. To know what it would be like to take everything he wanted. To explore all her softness. Her innocence.

That was the true shame. It was her innocence, his desire to tear off her armor and expose all that soft sweetness, that called to him and it was those very things that should keep him from ever touching her.

And yet, were she another woman, more jaded, more purposefully seductive, he doubted he would have felt a thing.

It was her differences. The very things that made her forbidden. That was what made her call to him.

"You really think they're missing something?" she asked.

"Yes," he said, knowing he should stop. Knowing he should cut her down as effectively as he'd just built her up. Something to get her to stop looking at him with those round blue eyes. Looking at him like he was some kind of hero.

"How can everyone have missed it, Ferro?" she asked. "What is it about me? I don't really go out of my way to hide the good things about myself. Why does everyone see something wrong with me? Why do people just want to take things from me?"

"The truth? I think you're too smart for most people. You're intimidating. And it's clear you wouldn't be able to connect with someone who isn't somewhat exceptional. You're a challenge, and that frightens some men. Or…makes them want to subdue it." She flinched when he said that. "Also, I think you don't really want any of the men who haven't shown interest in you. I think you're more in control than you think."

"Do you?"

"You're the kind of woman who knows how to go out and get what she wants. A billionaire before age twenty-one, a leader in the technology industry. An amazing feat for your age. Nearly unheard of for your gender. I think you're in much more control than you give yourself credit for."

Julia looked down into her champagne, and back up at Ferro. He was impeccably dressed, the lines of the custom suit skimming his physique, a physique she'd seen quite a lot of this morning. Ferro did a good impression of a man who was civilized, and yet, she knew he wasn't. Not really.

She'd seen beneath the suit this morning. And she was more than a little intrigued.

And he thought she had more control than she gave herself credit for. What would happen if she tried to seduce Ferro? If she went for what she wanted?

He wanted her, too. Well, maybe he did. He had kissed her like he was drowning and she was air back in California, and he'd said that those who didn't see why she was special were stupid. Which meant he had to think she was.

That was even beside the point. She didn't need for him to think she was special, she just needed him to want her.

She was ridiculous. A twenty-five-year-old virgin letting so many fears and insecurities hold her back. He was right. Her armor was total bull. She was still just living in fear, living to protect. She wasn't fortified by her image. She was hiding behind it.

But if she was with Ferro...she could break through the wall. This one big wall of fear that surrounded her. And he would make it crumble. Because Ferro Calvaresi was a master of the game. The kind of man who made women lose their minds for a chance to have his body.

There was a thought.

If you wanted to learn about a subject, you learned from a master. That was just common sense. So if she wanted to learn about sex...

She took a drink of her champagne. Fortification. Much needed. Then she took a step toward him and put her hand on his arm. "And do you like women who are in control?" she asked, going for a sultry tone, though she was pretty sure she sounded a little raspy.

Something in his eyes changed. Darkened. "No."

"Oh."

"I like to be in control."

Something about the way he said it, his voice smooth and rich, melting through her like warm chocolate, made her shiver. Opened up a craving in her that shocked her with its strength.

"Well, that's…that's too bad since…since you think I'm in control. But you like to be." She was botching the seduction. She should have known she would be lame at seduction.

And it sucked because she really did want him. Right now, she wanted him so bad that she ached with it. It was a new and terrifying experience. But it seemed…it seemed like she could do it, too.

With Ferro there would be no feelings, but there would be no games, either. There would be no demands, no force. He wouldn't trust her, he wouldn't ask her to trust him. They could give each other pleasure and then…and then go back to how things were.

"Could you…" She hesitated and then took a breath, plunging on. "Could you come out onto the balcony with me?"

"Looking for a repeat performance of our balcony visit in California?"

"If I was?"

"Are there reporters?"

"Probably."

He held his arm up and she curved hers around it, allowing him to lead her through the room and out onto the wooden terrace. Lanterns hung low in even intervals, casting glowing orbs out onto the lake below.

She took a breath and released it, watching as it lingered in the air, her eyes on the stars. So many stars. More than she'd ever seen before. This place was different. Wild. And she felt different and wild in it.

She turned to Ferro and put her hand on his face, searching his expression for clues. There was nothing there. He was stone. Unreadable, unknowable.

But she wasn't going to wait for his cue. She was going

to give her own. And exercise that control thing he seemed to think she had.

She put her other hand on the back of his neck, lacing her fingers through his hair. And then she closed her eyes, because looking at him didn't help, he was too handsome to be real, and leaned in, pressing her lips to his.

They were warm, firm. Immobile. So she changed the angle of her head, touched the seam of his mouth with the tip of her tongue.

And then he moved, his arm sliding slowly around her waist, drawing her in tight, crushing her breasts to his chest. He held her there, letting her kiss him, not returning it, not denying it.

"Kiss me," she said, her lips still pressed to his.

And for a moment, a blinding, blistering moment, he obeyed. His mouth moved over hers, so expert, so incredibly skilled. A shiver went through her body, arousal skating over her skin. The damp slide of his tongue creating an answering wetness between her thighs.

Oh, yes, she wanted him. She wanted him to show her everything she'd been missing.

Then he pulled away suddenly and the air, hitting her where his body had been before, left her chilled.

"What?" she asked.

"Nothing. But that's quite enough of a public display, don't you think?" He was breathing hard, she noticed, something he had not done after their kiss in California. And his face looked slightly flushed, hard to tell in the dim light, but she was sure she could see a faint slash of crimson across his sharp cheekbones.

Two things were suddenly apparent to her: he was aroused now. And the first time they kissed he hadn't been.

She wasn't totally sure what to feel about either thing.

"I suppose so," she said. Her own breathing was totally erratic, her heart pounding unevenly. And her legs were shaking.

He turned away from her and walked to the edge of the balcony, leaning down against the railing, his forearms resting on the rough-hewn wood.

She followed him, coming to stand next to him. "I want you," she said, the words coming out in a rush.

He didn't react, didn't move or look at her or anything. He simply stared out at the water.

"Ferro...I—I'm not asking for anything outside of this deal we have. I just want you. In bed. Until all of this is over, and then you walk away with what you want, and I walk away with what I want."

"A business transaction," he said, his tone hard and flat.

"Yes. What's wrong with that?"

He straightened. "I find I have no taste for things like this."

Hurt burned through her. Was it possible she'd misread him? That he didn't want her at all? The humiliation was a lot worse than she'd imagined it would be. Yeah, a lot worse. She just felt small all of a sudden. The awkward girl she'd always been.

But of course, she had nothing material to offer Ferro outside of the agreement they already had. So why would he even humor her?

"I'm sorry you find me so distasteful," she said crisply. And the hurt, anger, pent up from the past ten years of her life, and from her ridiculous encounter, earlier, with David Whatshisname and Ferro's rejection, built up and boiled over, words spilling out hot and reckless. "Should I have offered you money? Is that an exchange you understand?"

He pushed off from the balcony and turned to face her, his expression anything but blank now, dark eyes blazing with fire. "Careful, *cara mia.*"

"Forgive me, if I don't find it a little insulting that you,

Ferro Calvaresi, who everyone knows seduced rich older women for their money and status, finds sleeping with *me* to be distasteful."

He reached out and grabbed her arm, pulled her back up against him. For the first time, she saw him without any civility. The mask dropped completely. There was no more charm. No more easy smile. No more laughing, mocking playboy. This was the man from the street. The man who had put aside every ounce of morality in order to survive.

He said nothing, he only looked at her. Then he extended his hand and touched her cheekbone, traced a line down to her chin, his eyes never leaving hers. "So you want to talk about my past, do you? You think you understand it because you read a book? Did the details excite you? Stories of my exploits with past lovers? Did you like the part where they said I took a married woman back into the coatroom and had her against a wall while her husband was in the ballroom searching for her? That was my favorite."

She shook her head, the sense she'd gone too far making her freeze inside. "Ferro…I don't…"

"But you don't know the details of it. That makes for a hell of a salacious story. A young stud that women find irresistible. A rogue with no conscience who got gifts based on sexual skill. But that's sanitized, Julia. The clean version."

"It can't be…"

"Yes. It can be. I assume you know what a whore is."

She blinked, her chest suddenly tight. "Yes."

"I was hardly the cheerful seducer of lonely women I'm made out to be. I was paid to be there. In their beds. In the coat closet. I was a whore, Julia. Paid for sex. I sold my body to the highest bidder and I did whatever was asked of me, whether I wanted to or not."

"I can't… You couldn't have been. That's not…"

"You think I'm exaggerating, don't you?" he asked. "I'm

not. I was taken from the streets at sixteen by a woman named Claudia. She was wealthy, older. Looking for a little bit of fun. It had been four days since I'd eaten. I was looking for work but I could hardly stand. The first thing she did was buy me a meal. And after that…how could I say no to whatever she asked? I was starving for food, for touch, for a bed that wasn't dirt, so I went and I took her money gladly. But I was her pet, Julia. I learned to obey her every command, to be her fantasy lover. But that was never all she had in mind. She wanted to make money off me, too. And she had contacts, other women, women she knew would be willing to pay to have a young man in their bed who did everything they demanded. She taught me English. She taught me to dance. She taught me about art and culture and everything I would need to know to be a pleasing companion. Trained. Like an animal."

Julia swallowed, her stomach tight, sick.

"You want me to stop, don't you?" he asked.

She nodded. She did. She didn't want to know. Because until a moment ago he'd been a fantasy. And now it was far too real. Just hearing about it made her feel like she was covered in dirt. How must he feel?

"It's too bad, you baited me, now deal with the consequences. You want to talk about my past then you need to know what it really was. I took money for sex. I did whatever my lovers asked me to do and I did it well. I also listened when they talked. The wives of rich men know a lot about money. About investments. I figured out how to make the money I earned grow. It's hard to leave a lifestyle like that. Where you make hundreds of dollars for an hour's…work. But eventually it became clear to me that the cost was too high, and I don't exchange myself anymore. I am not for sale. I am not your pet you can make demands of. I am a man, and I have demands of my own."

She nodded slowly and backed away from him, breaking his hold on her. She turned and walked back into the ballroom, keeping her head down while she walked through the knot of people.

Her stomach felt like it had a brick in it. Her entire body shaking. How easy it had been to use the idea of his past to judge him. To make herself feel superior to him in some way. How easy it had been to use it against him. To make light of it.

Now she felt like she was being torn apart from the inside out. Felt like she'd been forced to look in on what he'd been through, with nothing to shield her from it.

Ferro was a proud man. And he'd had his pride stripped from him during that part of his life.

Had been forced to belong to other people.

It hurt her he'd been through it. And her vision of him changed. Not the worldly playboy, but the victimized boy. Sixteen and in desperate need of so many things. Of guidance and love, and shelter. And he'd been offered an empty version of those things and had latched onto them. But she saw him now, for what he was.

She'd imagined him as the smooth, suave womanizer. As the man who took gifts with a wink and left his lover sated and satisfied. She hadn't realized…she'd never imagined that he'd sold himself. His body.

And yes, it disturbed her. But it also made her feel some sort of a strange connection with him. Because she'd had a taste of how dehumanizing, how frightening and horrifying it was to have someone try to take possession of your body when you didn't want it.

Only he'd done it over and over again. Submitted to it. For survival. It made her ache.

It made her feel too exposed.

But he didn't want her anyway. And now she didn't blame him. She'd insulted him past the point of reason. She'd treated him like a whore and, now, knowing his past, she knew he had every right to hate her for it.

She pushed the button for the elevator, about nine times more than she needed to, then stepped in and leaned her head back against the wall, letting it carry her up to her floor. Maybe she should quietly get another room. Put some distance between them.

But she couldn't do that because if they got caught sleeping separately then the news of a split might come bite them in the butt and that was not what they needed before pitching to Barrows.

She was trapped. Still trapped in this hell of their own making.

She stepped off the elevator and stalked down the hall, sliding her card through the reader. It didn't go. "Argh!" She slid it again, and was met with a red light. "Oh, you stupid, stupid, stupid thing!" She slid it again. And again. And kicked the door. Then she forked her fingers through her hair and turned around, leaning against the wall, fighting against tears. Against overwhelming misery.

The elevator next to the one she'd just arrived in, opened and Ferro stormed out. He strode toward her, dark eyes locked with hers. He tugged at the knot of his tie and jerked it off his neck, letting it fall to the floor.

He stopped right in front of her, his hand braced on the wall behind her. He leaned in, his lips a whisper from hers. "Don't walk away from me."

"Or what?" she asked.

He wrapped his arm around her waist and pulled her against him. He lowered his hand from the wall and traced the outline of her lips with his thumb.

"You know my secrets now," he said.

She nodded slowly. "You broke your rule. Don't confirm or deny."

"I did. I am also breaking another rule."

"What's that?" she asked, her voice breathless this time for real.

"I want," he said. "I don't let myself want."

"You don't let yourself want…sex?"

"No. I have never had a lover, Julia, does that shock you?"

"But…but you said…I don't understand."

"I've had sex but I've never had a lover. I've had clients, not lovers. I have never been with a woman of my choosing, and whatever I have done in a bedroom has been controlled by the other person. I have learned, in those situations, to be nothing more than a body. I detached, as completely as possible, found a fantasy in my mind that allowed me to function and…that's it. I didn't have to think. I didn't have to feel. It's wasn't my body then. I didn't live in it."

"They all told you what to do?"

He shook his head. "I am an expert at reading people. I know what they want. What they need." He lowered his head for a moment. "I don't know what *I* want. I have never asked myself the question."

"And…and now?"

"I want you," he said, raising his gaze, his eyes locking with hers. "On my terms. If you want an arrangement, I'll give you one. You, in my bed until the deal is finalized at Barrows. In the end, when we part ways, perhaps if it is agreeable to you, you could take a slightly larger share of the product."

She shook her head. "No. I'm not letting you buy me. If you want me…if you want *me,* then maybe. But I want to be more than a convenience. More than just someone you thought you could get easily because of our situation. I don't want to be someone you feel…entitled to." It was the one thing she couldn't deal with. That he would feel like he owned her, this moment, for some reason.

"My confession has given you second thoughts?" He released his hold on her.

She bit her lip. "I could say no, but it would be a lie."

"Come inside." He pulled a card out of his pocket and slid it through the reader. It, of course, turned green and released the lock on the first try.

She followed him into the room. Her heart pounding hard, her legs shaking. Because she didn't know what he would get her to agree to. Her body ached. It wanted, regardless of what her mind thought.

He unbuttoned the collar of his shirt, then his sleeves, and turned to face her. It was dark in the room, except for one lamp by the bed, casting everything in a strange, dim glow that made it all seem unreal.

"If you decide you want me, then there would be rules."

"What rules?"

"You will learn to please me. You will learn what I want. And you will give it me. Your primary goal will be my pleasure. I have never had a lover, Julia, and now that I have decided to take one, it will be on my terms."

"And what about my pleasure?" she asked, privately thinking that no matter what he did, it would pleasure her.

She should be running the other way. This was so many leagues beyond her. A man like him, well-versed in sex, but with no idea how to please himself.

She didn't know how to please him, either. And she was a mass of total confusion. On the one hand, she was attracted to him. And that was probably clouding her judgment big time. But mixed with that was the desire to heal him. To give to him where all anyone else had done was take.

Because she understood. How desperately lonely it was when people only used you. And for him, so much worse. A lifetime spent alone on the street. Alone in bed with strangers. Alone at the top of his success.

She also understood how important it was to choose your lover. Part of her was relieved it was happening like this. Not in the heat of the moment, but with a pause for discussion. With a definitive answer from both sides. It made her feel powerful. Made her feel in control. She imagined Ferro felt the same, and shouldn't it be that way? Shouldn't both parties want it?

Maybe they could help each other feel less alone. If only for a little bit.

Added to that, being told what to do could only be a help to her. She was after experience, after all. After a little training. And it helped make her not feel quite so afraid of doing the wrong thing. If she was following orders, she couldn't mess it up.

It was on the tip of her tongue to tell him she'd never had a lover, either. But then she didn't. There wasn't enough room for both of their baggage. And she had a feeling that he was on the verge of sending her away. Of retreating into his rules, behind his walls of control.

"And what will you want from a lover?" she asked.

He began to pace, his hands clasped behind his back, his movements smooth and sleek, dangerous like a predatory cat. "Do you want to know? I will not smooth the truth for you. If you want this, you are agreeing to take me. All of me. As I am."

"Tell me first. Then I'll decide."

"I think my lover's pleasure is important to me," he said. "You are in luck there. I've no interest in taking without giving back."

As had been done to him. She finished the sentence in her head.

"I will expect you to learn what I like. To learn to give it without asking. You will follow my instructions."

"And if I don't want to do something you ask of me?" she asked.

He stopped walking, his eyes meeting hers. "My lover's pleasure is important to me," he said. "Always remember that."

It was on the tip of her tongue. To tell him she understood why this was important to him. To tell him she was a virgin. To tell him why. But she didn't.

Because she didn't want him to know, not now. She didn't want to feel vulnerable. She didn't want to feel disadvantaged. She looked up at Ferro, her eyes locking with his, and she knew, that with him she wouldn't feel that way.

He looked like a man possessed of a desire, a man held just as captive by this thing between them as she was. A man who was held by her power. By his need for her.

"If I say no?"

"Then nothing happens. After the position I was put in life, I would never want a lover who didn't want me. Desire me to the point of distraction. As I desired her."

And in that moment she felt strong. For the first time, just being her, having a man look at her, made her feel strong. It made her feel like she could give him this, give him the control, and that he would only reward her for it.

One thing was certain, physically, Ferro would never hurt her. And emotionally…he was her enemy. There was no chance at an emotional entanglement.

Perfect.

Her choice was made. For tonight, whatever he asked, her answer would be yes.

She sucked in a breath, her heart pounding, her stomach sick. "I agree to your terms."

CHAPTER NINE

FERRO CURLED HIS hands into fists to disguise the trembling in his fingers. His desire for Julia was raging out of control, far surpassing anything he'd ever felt before.

He'd confessed all to her. The unvarnished truth of his life. Still she said yes. Still she wanted him.

He found that the wanting was important. He knew that he wanted her, craved her like he couldn't remember craving anything in life beyond the essentials. Food, water, heat. And now Julia.

"Tell me," he said, the words rough, "that you want me."

She looked away, her cheeks turning pink. "I told you already," she said.

"You're already failing your directive. I asked you to do what I said. Tell me you want me."

She met his gaze. "I want you."

Touching her would be like touching fire. Just the thought made him warm.

He closed the distance between them and pulled her to him, his lips hovering over hers. "I will kiss you now," he said. "And this is not about restraint. Or seduction. Or control. This is for me. This is not for you, or for anyone else. It's not for any other reason than that you are a woman, and I am a man, and I want you like I have never wanted anyone or anything in my entire life."

The admission was shaky, frayed, and he didn't care. His control could burn in hell. And he would follow. Surely for this, he would follow.

He looked at her mouth, pink and lush, soft. Feminine perfection. He had stopped looking at the women he'd been with at a certain point. Had stopped truly looking at them. He saw past them whenever he could.

But he didn't want to see past Julia. If he was going to do this, he would embrace it utterly, as utterly as he'd embraced his control. He would let go of it with just as much purpose.

He leaned in, tracing the line of those gorgeous, rose-colored lips with his tongue. Tasting her, savoring her. She shivered beneath his touch, her bottom lip trembling, the art-less show of arousal pushing his up higher.

How long had it been since he'd wanted without shame? So long.

He didn't have to hide behind a fantasy to maintain his arousal. Didn't have to pretend he was in control, with a woman he wanted, somewhere he wanted to be.

He was the richest man in the world. He was just where he wanted to be, with the woman he wanted. He would savor each taste of her, every glimpse of her skin. The feel of her softness beneath his hands.

He deepened the kiss, delving into the recesses of her mouth, drowning in her. And she returned it. Enthusiasti-cally. Passionately.

He had a hundred fantasies. Locked away inside himself, his defense against the invasion of his body. The invasion of his soul.

They hadn't protected him completely, but they had given him a place to go.

The only question was, which one would he live out to-night, with her.

He bit her lip, testing her. Seeing what she would call a

stop to. What she would enjoy. The slight bite only earned him a whimper, one of desire, not pain.

"You like that?" he asked.

"Yes," she whispered.

"Good." He stepped away from her, took one last look at her in the dress. "Take that off. Slowly."

Her cheeks darkened, but she obeyed, reaching around behind herself. Her dress loosened, the top falling to her waist. She was wearing a black bra, plain and sexy, her breasts spilling over the low cups, so pale against the dark fabric.

"All the way," he said.

She tugged at the fabric around her hips and the dress fell away, a dark, shimmering pool at her feet. Then she stepped out of it, leaving her in nothing more than the bra, a very small pair of matching panties and her spiky shoes.

They made her legs look endless. He wanted them wrapped around his back. Yes, that would have to happen. A definite fantasy.

She didn't make a move to him. She just stood there, her body on display for him, awaiting her next order.

He moved to her, put his hand on her cheek. "You are so much better than beautiful."

"What does that mean?" she asked, her voice shaking.

"You are beautiful, but there is something in you. Something that shines from inside. That is what makes me want to lose control with you. Because I want to touch the light. I want to feel warm. You will make me feel warm."

Then she was pulling him to her, kissing him. There was something unrestrained in her, something totally different than anything in his past experience. She was hungry for him, but it wasn't in the same way other women had been with him.

She was just so very soft. Sweet, if anything so torturously sensual could be called that.

He sucked her tongue deep into his mouth, and she moaned, her fingers digging in to his shoulders.

He reached around and undid the catch on her bra, then slid his hands down her back, beneath the waistband of her underwear, cupping her bare butt. He squeezed her gently, enjoying her body, not simply giving it enjoyment.

Always for him, sex had been clinical. The go-to images in his mind keeping his body on track. But not now. Now, there was nothing that could have doused his arousal, no way to stop it from consuming him, leading him deeper and deeper down a dark path that he had to see through to the end. Even though he couldn't see in front of him. Even though he knew nothing good waited. Not past the oblivion that would come with release.

None of it mattered. All that mattered was her. Was this. Was getting what he wanted.

He pulled away from her and tugged at the front of her bra, drawing it down beneath her breasts, exposing her to him. She was so perfect. Pink and perfect. He lowered his head and slid his tongue over one nipple, felt it harden. Then he sucked her deep into his mouth, savoring her, the flavor, the way she arched into him, the way she grabbed his hair and held him to her body as though she couldn't bear to be separated from him.

All things that had disgusted him when it had been with a woman he didn't want. A woman he was, in some ways, forced to be with. With Julia, they made him burn. He craved more.

It was like a beast had been unleashed inside him, and after more than ten years of celibacy, more than ten years of starving himself, he was very, very hungry. He sucked her in deeper, before releasing it and turning his attention to the other breast, giving her the same attention there.

But it wasn't enough. He rose, claimed her lips again, then

he picked her up and held her close to his chest. She squeaked and held on to him tight, but didn't break the kiss. Her nails dug into his neck, a delicious bite of pain to go with the almost unendurable pleasure.

So delicious it ramped up his appetite all the more.

He deposited her on the bed and stood at the foot of it. "Lie down." She obeyed, sliding her bra off the rest of the way and holding still. "Part your thighs for me."

Again she obeyed. He knelt on the edge of the bed and let his fingers drift over her panties, rubbing her through the fabric.

Julia felt as if her heart was going to implode, it was beating so hard. And the pleasure, the absolute, raw unsatisfied, pleasure that was building in her was threatening to undo her completely.

She shouldn't respond to his orders like she was. She shouldn't want more of them. She should be completely put off dominant men. But she wasn't. And she did respond. Because she'd chosen him, chosen this. And she didn't have to worry about being awkward or wrong. He was telling her what to do. Exactly. His instructions explicit and exquisite. And she was happy to oblige.

She spent so much time giving orders. Having people defer to her, treat her gently. Well, Ferro was giving orders. And he wasn't gentle.

And she liked it. Oh, yes, she liked it.

His fingers slipped beneath the waistband of her underwear and found where she was wet and very, very ready for him. It was almost embarrassing, displaying just how much she wanted him. But then she looked at him, at the shocking and graphic outline of his erection against the front of his slacks, and she didn't feel so embarrassed anymore.

Because he wanted her, too. Because he wanted her as a lover when he'd wanted no other woman. Not for her money, not for her status. Not because her mom had paid him to be her date and felt like she owed him.

He'd called her more than beautiful, so it wasn't even just for her body.

Tears, stupid, stupid tears, stung her eyes and she blinked them back, focused instead on the feelings that were rioting through her body as he teased and tested her, each pass of his fingers becoming more and more intimate until he pushed one deep inside her body.

A sharp cry escaped her lips and her internal muscles pulsed around him. Nothing had ever felt so good. Who would have thought she could find something like this with a man she didn't even like.

That assessment didn't sit well with her anymore, though.

She thought back to their first kiss.

Make it my punishment.

"Is this my punishment?" she panted as she dragged her underwear down her legs and tossed them onto the floor.

He pressed a kiss to her stomach, just below her belly button. "I think it's mine," he said. "Because I'm sure I won't survive it."

He kissed her lower, then lower still, forcing her legs open with his shoulders. He curled his hands around her thighs and tugged her hard against him as he tasted her intimately, his lips and tongue teasing, torturing.

"Oh." She put her arm over her eyes, unable to think, unable to breathe. He felt so perfect. So unbelievably decadent. She moved her arm, looked down at him, at his dark head right there. "I thought...I thought I was supposed to pleasure you."

He lifted his gaze, met her eyes. "This pleasures me." He slid his tongue across her flesh, his focus still on her. "More than you can know. Because I want you. Because I chose you." He lowered his eyes and shifted, releasing his hold on one leg and sliding a finger inside her again, working in time with his mouth, pushing her higher, faster.

She was breathless, her chest seized up, the tension, low in her belly, tightening to a point beyond pleasure, beyond pain. It was unendurable. Unsurvivable.

And just when she was sure she would break, he moved his tongue over her one last time and it all broke into pieces. Pleasure, white hot waves of it, rolled through her, her body completely destroying everything in its path. Leaving it changed. Devastated.

Perfect.

And she wanted to cry. Because this was what sex was about. Not rough violence. Not hard hands between her legs, trying to force their way inside her body. Not insults or force.

She pushed her memories aside. They had no place here. This was different. This was what sex, foreplay, was supposed to be. They weren't even on the same planet as what had happened to her back in high school. So she wouldn't think of it again. Not here. Not now.

He moved away from her then, his eyes dark with desire. "Now—" he wrapped his hand around his shaft "—now my turn, I think."

She bit her lip and nodded. She wanted him. Wanted this. Ferro was a lover doubtlessly unmatched. She was learning from the best. But right now she couldn't think of it that way. She couldn't even think. She could only want.

"Condoms?" she asked, feeling panicked suddenly. "Please tell me…"

"The hotel has provided some. I saw them in the bedside drawer."

He went to the opposite side of the bed to the one she'd been sleeping on and pulled a drawer open, producing a box of protection and setting it on the nightstand.

He opened it and produced a packet, handing it to her. "Put it on me," he said, his voice rough.

And she couldn't deny him. Because it was an order. Because she could tell that beneath every order was a desperation that she didn't entirely understand, but that she couldn't ignore.

She opened the packet, hoping he didn't notice her shaking hands, and, after examining it to make sure she was holding it the right way, she positioned the condom over his length and rolled it onto him. He was so hot and hard beneath her hand. Different than she'd imagined a man would feel. Better.

And she wanted all of him. Wanted him inside her.

"What else would you like?" she asked, meeting his gaze, loving the darkness in his eyes, the heat.

"I want you on your back. And I want you to wrap your legs around my back."

She complied, her heart pounding furiously. He positioned himself, the head of him testing the entrance to her body. He pushed forward, starting to stretch her. It hurt a bit, no dramatic tearing, but not painless.

Her breath was sucked from her lungs when he thrust into her fully, buried to the hilt, so deep in her, his chest pressed against hers. It hurt. But that wasn't the dominant feeling. It was the intense connection. The feeling of being completely joined to someone else, almost like she was a part of him.

"Julia…"

"I'm fine," she said, kissing the corner of his mouth, his cheek. "I'm fine. Please. Just…please."

He reached beneath her and cupped her butt, drawing her in tighter. And she did as she was told, wrapped her legs around him as he started to move in her. Each thrust brought his body into contact with the sensitive bundle of nerves at the apex of her thighs. Each thrust drove her higher, closer to another release.

It should be impossible after such an explosive orgasm, but he was taking her there. Too fast. Too intense.

She bit her lip, trying to hold back the groan of pleasure climbing her throat, trying to stop the rising tide of release that was threatening to wash her away completely.

But there was no holding either one back.

She held on to him as the storm took hold, and as she shuddered out her last gasp of pleasure, Ferro stiffened above her, his muscles shaking as his own release pounded through him, as he spent himself completely.

She clung to him, held his head to her chest, their breaths harsh, her heart beating hard. She could feel his against her body, in rhythm with hers.

He rolled away from her and sat up, the muscles in his back shifting with the movement. He put his head down, his face in his hands for a moment before he threw the blankets aside and stood quickly.

He went into the bathroom and closed the door behind him.

Julia sat up, drew her knees to her chest and waited. He didn't reappear. After a while she picked her phone up and started playing a game, trying to ignore the pressure that was building in her chest. She heard the shower turn on and blinked rapidly. She shouldn't be crying. She shouldn't even be tempted to cry. This was a learning experience. She and Ferro were lovers. Nothing more. If he wanted to roll out of bed without saying a word and take a shower by himself, then he was welcome to. Fine and fine.

She shivered and set her phone down, then got out of bed and went to her suitcase. She'd tossed her sweats onto the top of it when she'd gotten up that morning. A morning that seemed like it had happened days and days ago. Or in an alternate universe.

She'd crossed over the veil, into some strange place where hot men like Ferro noticed her, wanted her, took her. She jerked her T-shirt on, then started working on her pants. Oh, yes, then after that they left her cold and alone in bed.

If it was an alternate universe, it had some striking similarities to the usual one. And she wasn't all that thrilled about it. Because yeah, the hot dude had wanted her. But only for a little bit.

She climbed back into the bed. It smelled like him. Like sweat. Like sex. She wished he would just come back and put his arms around her for a moment, because after being so close to him, after having him in her like that, she felt more alone without him than she ever had.

Why did she feel like this? Why was it…why was it making her shake and get teary eyed? Why did she want to eat a pint of ice cream and hide?

For a blinding moment, during the sex, she'd thought she finally understood it. How beautiful it was. Pleasure, the wanting, the being wanted. That she'd finally cut the link between her assault and sexual desire. Really, and not just in theory.

Well, that was true, but she'd found a whole new level of complexity in this sort of thing she hadn't anticipated at all.

But she held her tears back, and she sat and stared at her phone screen, mindlessly flicking letters into slots. None of them were words, and therefore, pointless. She was starting to wonder if the little experience with Ferro had been the same.

Except she felt changed. Burned from the inside out. Damn Ferro.

The bathroom door opened and she tried to keep herself from getting whiplash, looking to see what he was going to do. What the expression on his face was.

She managed to look up from her phone slowly. He wasn't looking at her at all.

He had a towel slung low around his hips, and he stalked across the room to the closet, where he had hung all his clothes. He was meticulous, much more so than her. Everything he did was purposeful. Controlled.

Except for what he'd done tonight.

He dropped the towel and her heart climbed into her throat, perched there, blocking her air, pounding so hard she felt dizzy. She'd never seen a butt like that. Well, outside of pictures she'd never seen a man's butt uncovered. Even so, she knew he was a rare specimen of extreme hotness. And even though she was irritated and hurt, she couldn't help but look.

He tugged a pair of athletic pants out of the closet and jerked them on, covering the object of her fascination. Then he turned and started to walk toward the couch.

He still didn't look at her, didn't say anything.

He lifted up the blankets and lay down, turning over, facing away from her.

Her mouth fell open. Was he really going to just go to sleep across the room from her as if nothing had happened between them?

She stared at his immobile form. Well. Damn. He was.

She started to say something. Then she closed her mouth. If she said something he would know that she was melting inside. And she couldn't take that humiliation, not again. She'd been so blithe about a guy using her for her body.

But she hadn't known what it would really feel like. That she would feel so used.

She hadn't known anything.

She'd been so stupid. To think that because she'd wanted the sex she'd have no emotional repercussion from it. To think that because Ferro was her business rival it wouldn't change her feelings. To think that she wouldn't feel rejected and hurt if he didn't want to sleep next to her.

She forced herself to lie down. Forced herself to keep quiet. But no matter how hard she tried she couldn't force herself to fall asleep.

CHAPTER TEN

FERRO SLUNG HIS bag over his shoulder and waited at the foot of the stairs. Waited for Julia to board the plane. She was stiff. Everything about her. Her nose was pointed straight toward the sky, her posture rigid, every step locked like a soldier's. And she was pointedly not looking at him.

And he supposed he deserved it. Thankfully, in the cold light of day with his control firmly back in place he could deal with her in a rational manner. Except, she wasn't being rational. Maybe he hadn't handled the night before the way that she wanted him to handle it, but he'd more than given her pleasure. He hadn't taken advantage in any way.

She ascended the stairs, keeping that same posture, never once looking in his direction, and he followed. He blew out a breath before entering the plane and watched it linger in the air. It was cold. Strangely he didn't feel it so much.

He sat on the couch across from her and she pulled her computer out, typing furiously, never once glancing at him all through takeoff.

"Are we having a problem, Julia?" he asked.

Her head snapped up. "Are you speaking to me again?"

"You're the one ignoring me," he said, struck by the oddness of the conversation. It sounded like a fight two people in a relationship, albeit a high school relationship, might have.

And he'd never had a relationship before, neither was this a relationship, so that made it all doubly odd.

"I am not!" she said, setting her laptop aside. Then she bit her lip and picked it back up, put the computer back on her lap and turned her focus back to the screen, her cheeks pink.

He'd never in all his life dealt with something like this.

She set her computer down again and looked back at him. "Why did you sleep on the couch last night?"

"Why would I not sleep on the couch?"

"Because we…shouldn't you sleep together after sleeping together? I assumed that was where that highly glossed term came from."

"I've never slept with a woman I had sex with."

"You've never had a lover before, either, remember? It was supposed to be different."

A strange pang struck his chest, worked its way through his body. "In that I was in control, and not the other way around. I'm not going to pick a China pattern out with you."

"I didn't ask you to. I just thought maybe you could say a few words to me. Or…get in bed with me. Why are you making me feel needy for asking for what, I'm sure, is bare minimum sex etiquette?"

"Did you not listen to anything I told you?" he asked, the burning in his chest getting worse. As it had been just after he'd finished with her last night. A virgin. She'd been a virgin. It had excited him. Made him feel some sort of masculine pride he'd been completely unfamiliar with until that moment.

And it had made him feel every inch the predator. Had made me feel no different than the women who had used him. At least they had given him something in return.

He would, though, regardless of what she said she wanted. He would make sure she was compensated for her time in his bed. For giving him her innocence.

"I listened," she said, her lips pulled tightly together.

"But you apparently didn't understand. If you wanted tenderness and feeling you should have picked a man who was capable of giving it to you. I can't. I don't want to. I want to make you come, and that's the beginning and end of it. If you can't handle that, then I'm not the man for you to stretch your sexual muscles with."

Slashes of dark color appeared on her cheeks. Anger, he could see, not embarrassment. She was shaking with it. Good. Maybe if he made her angry enough it would erase the hurt she felt, because he didn't know another way to do it. Didn't know how to offer comfort.

"I knew that with you all I was getting was good instruction. I knew you weren't going to want anything else from me. I just wanted a little quality training before I took another lover, but I damn well expected you to treat me with a little respect."

Such irony that she should speak of respect when she admitted she was using him for training. That she was using him the way the other women had.

As if he wasn't using her. Using all that sweet innocence as a salve for his bloody soul. But it was really just putting butter on a burn. All it did was hold the heat in so it burned faster and deeper.

"I am not the man for you, Julia, not even for temporary purposes. And I'm not training you." He spat the words out. "I'll do business with you, but this is over."

"Fine by me. I wouldn't let you touch me again. Not after the way you treated me last night."

"Then we've arrived back at the same place we've always been," he said.

"And that is?"

"Barely tolerating each other but prepared to work together if it will benefit us. No harm, no loss. Except your virginity, that is."

He didn't know what had possessed him to strike out at her. He only knew that the same feelings he'd been wrestling with since last night were threatening to rise up and strangle him again. That venting them this way seemed to stop them.

"Oh, classy, thanks, bring that up."

"You should have."

"Why? Why should I have to tell you? You said yourself we were just having a fling. You wanted to experience having the control, I wanted to learn from the best. We were both in it for ourselves, but that's life, isn't it? Everyone's in it for what they get out of the deal. I know those women used you, but you used them, too. You used them for money."

"The power differential was not in my favor, Julia, just trust me on that."

"I'm not saying it was but…"

"I was sixteen, I thought, yeah sure, get paid to have sex. I'd never in my life worried about sex much since I was too busy trying to figure out where my next meal would come from, or trying to teach myself to read so I could navigate my way through the world. But being a teenage boy, I was interested. With all my bravado, compliments of life on the street, I figured it wouldn't matter to me. That it wouldn't mean anything. And I was still a virgin so…it was even tempting on that level. But I didn't realize what it cost. What I would have to do to get through it in the end. Until you've been through it, you don't really understand, Julia. Until you've gone so far as to sell yourself to live, you don't know what it's like. Every time was like…having more and more of my skin stripped off until…at the end, I couldn't bear to have anyone touching me. It was torture. Not pleasure."

Julia looked down, some of her rage cooling then. In some ways she did understand. She hadn't realized how she would feel after sex. The rush of jumbled emotion that would hit her. She hadn't had a clue. And she pictured him as a teenager, innocent in that way, being led into something he couldn't possibly have understood the repercussions for.

"You can't stop when you start," he said. "Because there's no other way to make that kind of money in that little bit of time. Otherwise I was doing hard labor for twelve hours of the day and still not making enough to sleep in a bed at night. Not making enough to keep you fed, to keep up your strength to work."

"Ferro…"

"No, it's good you know. But I think it draws a line under the fact that you and I can't allow our personal attraction to have a place in this."

"Are you attracted to me?" she asked.

"I am. But I think you can now attest to the fact that being used for your body doesn't feel much better than being used for your money."

"I knew more about that than you might think. That wasn't being used, trust me. I didn't particularly enjoy the…after stuff, but the sex was great. I felt desired, I felt pleasure. I hope you did, too. I hope you didn't feel like I used you, because that wasn't what I wanted. Because whatever you might think, I do know that pain."

"Maybe we should just call the conversation over," he said.

"Oh, right. Over." So he didn't want her to share. Fine. She didn't want to share anyway. Things just weren't working out, and they were ending them. Which was the only way it was ever going to go.

But you don't want him anyway. Too much baggage. Not enough cuddling. Failed experiment. Back to the drawing board.

She sighed and looked back down at her computer, more than ready to just deal with some silence on the flight. It was better than this awkward conversation.

And she would try to ignore the fact that when she looked

at him, her body burned. There was no place for that. She'd made a mistake, but at least it had been her choice. And it wouldn't be terminal.

They were in a business relationship and it was time for her to remember that. Time to get back to California. Back to real life. Back to business.

"Why is there a giant metal salmon in my office?" Julia walked out into the foyer, coffee clutched in her hand, and over to Thad's desk.

"I thought you ordered it," he said, not looking at her and sounding way too innocent.

"You did not. Did Calvaresi come in and flash his abs at you?"

"I'm not that easy, Julia, honestly. You wound me."

She leaned forward, hands planted on Thad's desk. "And you let him put a fish in my office."

"It's not a real fish."

"Thad, focus."

"I thought since you were, you know, with him now, that it would be acceptable."

She was about to say she wasn't with him, but she couldn't say it, because she just remembered the assumption had been that they were together before they'd actually slept together and that the ruse had to go on with the absence of actual sex.

It was officially so complicated. And she was so damn trapped! Stupid media. Stupid Facebook page. Stupid, stupid celebrity nickname! JulErro. Of all the ridiculous…

And it was only getting worse. There was a website now. With unauthorized merch. Little joke T-shirts showing his phone breeding with hers and making sleek sparkly phone babies that possessed tech superpowers. So dorky. And if it hadn't been about her she would have thought it was hilarious.

"Assume that if Ferro wants to put anything in my office

other than flowers, he's messing with us both." She turned and stormed back into her office, dialing Ferro as she went.

"Why the fish, Calvaresi?" she said when he answered.

"Why not? You liked it."

"I was making conversation. How did you get it in here? How am I supposed to get it out?"

"That's rude, Julia, you make it seem like you don't like my gift."

The whole conversation was so strange. And so from a few weeks ago. He was back to being obnoxious Ferro, of the charming grins and zero depth. And she wasn't sure what she thought of that. On the one hand, it was a nice thought. Like they could erase that night in Alaska just by pretending it didn't exist. That all that honesty, that being skin to skin, hadn't happened.

On the other hand, in the week since their return, she'd thought of very little else. And everything about her felt different. She was more aware of every part of her body. Maddeningly aware. When she took a shower, she turned herself on just by trying to get clean. Because her mind automatically went to the way Ferro's hands had felt on her. The way the wet heat of his mouth had felt at her…

Her face burned and she turned her focus back to the salmon statue. "It can't stay here. I have to meet with people here."

"And what's wrong with a little natural art?"

"Bah!" She hung up the phone and threw it onto the low, cushy chair she had in the corner. Then she stalked to her desk and plopped down on the computer chair, her head rested on her hands.

Her desk phone rang. She answered it. "Julia Anderson."

"I'm going to need to see your idea from the Barrows pitch ASAP."

"Ferro, I just hung up on you."

"I know. But that was a personal call."

"Is a call about a fish statue really a personal call?"

"In this instance. And this is a business call. So, not the same."

She growled. "Whatever, man. Why don't you come by my office and…"

"No. Your office is a little crowded."

She gritted her teeth. "Now it is."

"So come to mine. Two hours. There will be lunch. And coffee. I'll see you then." He disconnected the call and Julia sat back in her chair, trying to order her thoughts. She was going to see Ferro for the first time since flying back from the wedding. She was going to have to figure out some kind of game face so that she didn't just blush, stammer and lose all the social grace she'd managed to train herself to have.

She took a sip of coffee and stared at the metal fish statue. Then burst out laughing. It was pretty funny. The ultimate inside joke.

As suddenly as the laughter had burst from her, it died. It would be funny if Ferro weren't using it as some sort of deflection. She wasn't stupid. He had regressed to the way they'd treated each other before the deal. Before the sex. And there was a reason for that.

Probably the same reason he'd shut down completely after their night together. Why he'd gone into the bathroom and showered for the better part of an hour before lying down and going to sleep without another word spoken to her.

She was just going to play it cool. Yep. Play it cool. She'd learned to do that as a way to protect herself from this kind of thing and she was just going to keep doing it.

Time to get her game face on.

* * *

Ferro didn't know what to expect from Julia when she came breezing into his office fifteen minutes later than he'd asked her to arrive.

She was wearing a black top with a rigid, ruffled collar that skimmed her jawline, black, feathered earrings dropping down inside it and disappearing into her top. Her pencil skirt, also black, was just as severe, as were her extremely high heels and the tight bun she'd tamed her blond hair into.

No soft pinks and golds in her makeup today. Thick liner around her eyes and lipstick like a ripe, black cherry made her look like she was ready to ride into battle. Ms. Julia Anderson had come to meet him in full armor today.

"Hello, Ferro, how has your day been? No steel aquatic creatures in your office I see."

"Not my thing."

"Right. Well. I've brought my ideas for the navigation system." She reached into her leather bag, also black, and pulled out her tablet computer, bringing up a three dimensional model on the screen. She turned it with her finger, showing different angles, the dimensions for each part of the system, fading in and out depending on what she was featuring.

"It will be touch screen. And voice activated. It will be able to look things up by landmark or by street, state, zip code, whatever. It will be especially handy when you're lost, and say, you're on Third Street, but you need to get to the wharf. So you can push a button on your steering wheel, activate voice recognition and say, 'How far am I from the wharf?' And it can tell you and map a route."

"Good ideas," he said. And they were. Julia did have a way of thinking like the kind of person who would need to use this piece of technology.

It was harder for him. Maybe because he didn't understand people especially well. Not normal, functional people.

They spent the next few hours altering her rendering, discussing features, modifying specifications and fighting over things one of them found necessary and the other felt was useless.

He couldn't remember the last time he'd enjoyed the conception of a product so much. And it had to do with Julia. With the fact that she felt so deeply about what it was they were doing. It made him want to put more into it. To match what she was giving.

By the time they were finished, there were five empty cartons on his desk that had once contained Chinese food, and they were on their fourth pot of coffee. And the sun had gone down, their afternoon meeting extending long past work hours.

"This is it!" Julia said, standing up from her position at his desk. "They're going to choose our design. How can they not? It's genius. Beyond genius, if I say so myself. I mean, really."

When it came to work, Julia was unable to disguise her passion all the way. And he was glad. She tapped into a part of herself, a part of life, that was off-limits to him. Watching her, being near her when she was overflowing with energy and exuberance was intoxicating.

Nearly as much as sleeping with her had been. No, he wasn't going there. He was determined to put that out of his mind. To forget it happened. It opened up too many doors he simply didn't want opened. Let in too many ghosts from his past.

And it almost felt like it might be worth the cost. Almost.

"It is a good design," he said, trying not to betray his thoughts. Trying not to show just how badly he wanted to push her onto his desk and have a repeat experience of what it was like to have sex on his own terms. With a woman he wanted. Wanted so much it made him burn.

"It's an amazing design."

"I think that should be all, then," he said, standing and straightening a stack of papers on his desk. Something to keep his hands busy, to keep from touching her. She was like fine porcelain, and he was afraid his hands were far too rough from all his years on the street. He had been foolish to think he could touch her without breaking her.

Foolish to think he could play with sex again and walk away unaffected. It never worked that way. It was why he hadn't gone there again since escaping Rome. Not until Julia.

And he wouldn't do it again. Not with her. There would be another woman, one who wouldn't challenge him so much. One who wouldn't make him feel like he was being torn apart from the inside out.

"That's…all?" she asked, her blue eyes round.

"Yes. There's nothing more for us to discuss today. We can pitch this to Barrows in person next week. Until then, we can both get back to our businesses."

Julia only stared at him, her mouth parted slightly, her cheeks flushed. And then she reached out and grabbed his tie.

CHAPTER ELEVEN

JULIA WASN'T QUITE sure what possessed her. Only that she'd been waiting, their entire eight hours together, for Ferro to give some indication that he remembered sharing the most intense and intimate moments of her life with her. But he'd refused.

He'd been cold, and when he hadn't been cold, he'd been that perfect brand of fake charming that she'd identified as such from moment one.

And he was trying to pull it on her again. Like he really was the womanizer that the press made him out to be. Like she didn't know the truth about him.

Like she didn't know the man had never had a partner who hadn't paid cash for him. Like she hadn't been his first lover.

And she couldn't take it anymore. One minute, she was standing a perfectly respectable distance from him, and the next, she was lunging at him, her hand wrapped around his silk tie.

He had the decency to look shocked for a split second. And that second was all she needed. When his mouth opened, she pulled hard on his tie and angled her head, pressing her lips to his and thrusting her tongue in deep. Tasting him. Punishing him.

His arms wrapped tight around her waist, pulling her close to him. She could feel him hardening, lengthening against her stomach. Her internal muscles clenched in response, an ache building where she longed to be filled by him again.

She pulled at the knot on his tie and it loosened. She pulled again, undoing it completely, and throwing it to the floor. She unbuttoned the top of his shirt, and continued on without asking, without checking his face.

He could stop her if he wanted. He would have to. Because she couldn't stop herself. She wanted him. With everything she had in her, she wanted him, and she didn't want to let him hide behind that facade he'd built up.

She wanted him real. She wanted him raw. She wanted him naked. And that wanting, that need, unblocked, unchained, no more fear holding her back, felt like the most delicious freedom she'd ever tasted.

She felt like Julia. Not like Julia who had been told she was wrong. Not like Julia who had been told she should be thankful for her attempted rape, because no other man would want her. Not like Julia who had been hiding behind her armor.

She was just Julia. Who she would have been without all of that garbage. Without all that pain.

Finally she had his shirt open, her fingers skimming along his perfectly defined muscles, his chest hair tickling her palms.

She wasn't taking orders today. She wasn't afraid of being clumsy. And when she looked at his face, his expression taut, his eyes nearly black, she wasn't afraid of being rejected, either.

She pushed his shirt off his shoulders and leaned in, pressing a kiss to his pectoral muscle before sliding her tongue around his nipple. He jerked beneath her touch and she smiled, kissing his skin again.

The way he responded to her now was completely different than after their first kiss. He'd been calm then, unruffled. Now, he wasn't. His heart was raging, his erection hard. There was no pretending that their night together hadn't changed things.

No way for him to pretend he was in absolute control. No way at all.

She had the control. But all she wanted to do with her control was pleasure him. Until he was shaking, until he was sweating. Until he was begging.

She dropped to her knees in front of him and started to work at his belt. Her fingers were trembling now. She'd never done this before, but she wanted to. She'd wanted to that first night they were together, and she would have, if he hadn't gone to the couch.

"You kept me from living out all my fantasies that night we were together," she said, sliding her hand over his cloth-covered shaft before undoing the button on his pants and lowering the zipper. "You won't deny me again."

She didn't know where the confidence was coming from. Didn't know who this woman was, with her hand wrapped around a man, with every intention of tasting him, having her way with him. She didn't know who this woman was, but she liked her.

And then she realized, this woman was her. The real her.

He reached up and grabbed her bun, tugging her hair, pulling her head back so she had to meet his eyes. "You think not?" he growled.

"I think I have you in the palm of my hand." She squeezed him and a feral groan escaped his lips, rumbling through his body. "You're mine, Ferro Calvaresi."

She reached beneath the waistband of his underwear and freed him, her fingers curled around his bare, heated flesh.

She leaned in and ran her tongue along the length of him, a shiver working its way through her body. She'd never felt so powerful. Had never felt so supremely comfortable in her own skin. On her knees, in front of a man, she might seem like she was the submissive. But she knew she had the control here. That she'd taken it from him. A good thing, because he badly needed the control stripped from him.

Ferro looked down at Julia, pleasure ripping through him. He was lost. He was past the point of regaining control in the situation. Past the point of thought and reason. He was lost in his needs, in the pounding, insistent need for release, and the need for her to keep going forever.

As she took him deep into her mouth, he lost the capability to think. To breathe. No woman had done this for him before. It was the ultimate in giving pleasure, while taking none. And she did it as though she could feel what he was feeling. As though she was just as lost in it all.

But he wasn't in charge here. He was at her mercy. And it felt like he was hurtling toward the edge of a cliff, with no choice but to go over. Flame roared through him, pushed him further, faster, dangerously close to the edge.

"Enough," he bit out. "Julia, I can't last."

She moved away from him, her face pink, her eyes bright. "Okay," she said, her breathing labored.

He moved to her then, undoing the buttons on her top while she finished discarding his pants and underwear. "I have no protection," he said.

"I, uh…I do."

"You do?"

"Thad," she said. As if her assistant's name explained things.

"What?"

"He slipped some in my purse before I left. He wants to make sure I play safe. And of course I couldn't tell him that we weren't…because he has to think we are. And anyway, now we are."

She shoved at the center of his chest and his legs gave easily, his body sinking into his office chair. Julia pulled her shirt off the rest of the way and unhooked her bra, tossing it to the side. Then she shimmied out of her skirt, leaving her in a pair of black panties and heels.

He'd thought a more vampish image would make her less appealing to him. He was wrong. He liked her like this. Aggressive, sexy. She pushed her panties down and kicked them to the side, then started on her shoes.

"Leave them," he said.

Her face turned pinker, and she smiled. "Okay." Then she reached into her purse and produced the condoms, walking to him slowly, her hips swaying. She was the very image of temptation. Of all the things he'd been denying himself for so long.

He was tired of denial. He just wanted to feel her, tight and wet around him, pushing him to release.

He didn't need a fantasy to stay hard for her. She was the fantasy.

She opened the protection and slid it onto his length, her fingers clumsy, delicate and arousing. "I'm hoping this will work," she said, putting one knee to the side of his thigh and gripping his shoulders, then bringing the other knee up alongside his other leg.

He put one hand on her lower back, the other around his erection, guiding himself into her body as she lowered herself onto him slowly.

Her hold on him tightened, her head falling back. "Oh, yes, this works."

He couldn't speak. He could hardly breathe. He had never wanted with such intensity. Had never had the arousal in his body mirror the desires in his heart like this. It was intoxicating. It was dangerous. And he didn't care.

He clung to her while she rode him, pushed them both higher. He lifted his face, caught her nipple between his lips and sucked her in deep, the hoarse cry that escaped her mouth sending a shock of need through him.

His lowered his hand, gripped her butt. The answering tightening of her hold on him, told him that she liked it.

And then he couldn't think anymore at all. His control was back in the distance and he didn't care. He could do nothing but feel. Could do nothing but chase his release, the pleasure blinding, burning, ravaging old scars and laying them open.

He felt like he was being torn to pieces. She arched into him, her internal muscles pulsing around him. No, this wasn't like being torn to pieces. That had already happened. His mind and body, his emotions, torn raggedly, violently into separate entities so that he could survive the indignity of his life. Survive the shame.

Here and now, it was like being forced back together. Cauterized and sealed by heat. Painful. Intense. Undeniable.

And with his name on her lips, she came, her nails digging into him hard, her eyes closed tight, her entire body rigid. And he could do nothing but follow, his blood raging in his ears as he poured himself out, spent himself. And when it was over, he was left hollowed out and breathless, savaged by the flame that had just burned through him.

He started to move and her fingers dug into his shoulders again. "No. Stay. Don't leave me. Please."

"Julia…"

"I need you."

And because no one had ever needed him before, he stayed.

Julia's breathing slowly normalized as she say curled against Ferro's bare chest. She had really, truly, just jumped him in his office, with the door unlocked. And she had really, truly, begged him to stay and clung to him like she was a koala bear.

And she was still clinging. She didn't know what had come over her. No, she did know. He'd been so calm. Acting like nothing at all had happened between them and so she'd wanted to make it so he couldn't ignore her. Couldn't deny that something had happened, that things had changed. Because she felt altered. Completely and utterly altered and the fact that he didn't just…sucked.

"I… Oh." She stood up, and almost fell back down again. All the blood had now rushed to her head and her thighs felt like overcooked noodles, thanks to the workout she'd just gotten. "I don't know what… I just… I did that."

Ferro was still sitting there, naked at his desk. She had to turn away from him because looking at him was making her all hot again.

"Don't ever apologize for your passion, Julia," he said.

She turned to face him, her heart thundering. "I don't."

"You do. It's beautiful. Don't apologize for it."

"This is…incredibly awkward. I don't really know what to say to the guy I just sort of attacked."

"Let me make a deal with you, Julia," he said, leaning forward.

"What sort of deal?" She started hunting for her clothes, knowing she couldn't just stand there all naked like it was casual and whatever. She was so *not* casual and whatever about being naked beneath the bright lights of Ferro's office.

"I will teach you," he said. "And you will accept my offer for a larger share of the Barrows deal."

"No. I don't want to deal like that."

"I do. I need it, Julia. In exchange, you will be my lover."

"We talked about this in Alaska."

"But you denied me my terms, and I can't have that. Neither can I seem to keep my hands off you. It's unacceptable. That means this attraction has to be allowed to run its course. I need my control, Julia."

"Ferro, I don't think I can do that."

"Trading your body is beneath you, *cara mia?*"

"But I would be with you for nothing."

"Everything has a price, that's how life works. That's how I understand it."

There was something horribly cold in his eyes, where before there had been heat. Something disconnected when for a moment she'd felt so close to him.

"Use me, Julia. I am offering to let you use me."

"As you'll use me?" she asked.

"Yes. But it is still not a balanced trade."

"Why not?"

"The one with the power in bed, the one making the commands, is always in control. And I will give you your due for allowing me this."

"But I want it," she said. "I want it like that. It's part of you teaching me."

"It's still not the same. This is…beyond me. Beyond my experience. I want you so much it makes me ache. I have never wanted like this. Always for me it's been survival. When I bought things for my office, it was because I could. A way of proving that I could have everything those women had in their homes, those women who were so superior to me. Everything that was in shops that barred my entrance could belong to me now. That I owned a part of the world that did such damage to me. But it wasn't because I wanted it. I hate this trash. Gaudy, pretentious. Utterly meaningless." He moved his hand in a sweeping gesture and brushed a plaster bust off his desk, onto the hard floor where it shattered.

"It is nothing," he said. "I didn't want it, I wanted what it represented. You, you I want. You are the first thing I have ever wanted. I will have you, Julia, if I have to work to find your price, I will have you and damn my soul."

Even though the coldness remained, the disconnect, she could sense more, a fire burning beneath the surface. Trying to melt the ice.

"You think I would cost you so much?"

"I know you will," he said. "But I don't care. Why do you want me?" he asked. "I am…there is dirt on my skin that will not come clean. Why would you touch me?"

"Because I don't see you that way."

"How?"

"You think I'm innocent, Ferro, because I was a virgin, but innocence and virginity aren't the same thing. I was a virgin because I was afraid, not…not so much of sex but the trust I would have to give in order to have it."

They were still naked, and that seemed right. It seemed appropriate that she should be naked while she told him this story because it made her feel exposed. Made her lower her armor. Made her strip herself completely.

She'd thought being with Ferro would be perfect because all she'd have to give was her body, and never herself, but she saw now that it wasn't enough.

"When…when I was in high school, I got this idea that I might like to go to prom. And my mother was thrilled because it was the first time I'd shown an inclination toward being 'normal.' All she'd ever wanted was a daughter who cared about shopping and boys, but I just wanted to program text-based adventure games and reenact fantasy battles in the park with other geeks. As you can imagine, no one was lining up to be my date. But right before the dance, Michael Coleman asked me to be his date. I said yes. He was handsome and popular and it seemed too good to be true. It was, by the way. It was too good to be true."

She swallowed. She hadn't realized how hard it would be to tell the story. She'd never told anyone, not the whole thing. "We spent hours choosing the dress. It was very pink. It was like bubblegum. And my date was handsome. He danced with me, spent time with me. It was great. And then…after the dance we got in the limo my parents had rented for us and he started… He kissed me, only I'd never kissed a boy before and he was going too fast. I asked him to stop and he wouldn't. He tore my dress, grabbed my breasts. He was so rough and it all just hurt. And I can't even explain how he looked. Like he was angry at me. Like he blamed me. And I kept saying no, but he kept going and he pushed my dress up and put his hand between my legs. And I hit him. As hard as I could. In the nose. Then he hit me across the face with the back of his hand. My nose was bleeding and…and then he said 'you stupid bitch. I was doing you a favor. No other guy would ever touch you. You should be thanking me. I'm only here because your mom paid me to be. After forcing me to dance with you all night I deserved to have you put out.' That was when the limo driver realized something was happening and intervened. He didn't…call the police or anything he just unrolled the divider and had me come up to the front seat. It's amazing how little people do in those situations, because no one wants to believe it happened."

"*Dio,* Julia that's…"

"That's why I don't see dirt on you, Ferro, because I understand what it feels like to have someone else try to own your body, to have someone act like they have a right to you. I understand that you were a victim."

"I wasn't."

"He told me I should thank him, Ferro. Because no other man would ever want to touch me. He told me I should thank him for holding me down and trying to force his way into my body. Should I have thanked him?"

"*Cazzo.*" Ferro's voice was rough, raw. "No, Julia. Of course not."

"How is it any different? She held food and shelter over your head. Your very survival. And I'm sure she acted like you should be grateful, or like you were business partners, or whatever she made you believe, but you don't have to thank the person who abused you. She could have just given you money, if she cared she could have. She could have put you to work in her kitchen, but instead she took a sixteen-year-old boy and demanded the use of his body, sold his body. I fail to see how you, as a boy, had any more control than me at sixteen in the back of that limo."

"But you punched his face. You walked away."

"I had somewhere to go."

"It doesn't matter…it doesn't make it okay."

"No. Not for either of us. Especially not for you. But we were the victims here. And it's a horrible word, I know. I hate it, but it's the truth. I want you to know I look at you and I see a man who earned his success. A man who deserves everything he has. A man who doesn't deserve to be defined by what he did to survive."

"A nice thought, Julia, but even if I believed I didn't need to be defined by it, I can't simply make it go away."

"I know that, too."

He leaned forward. "I would kill him. I want you to know that. Any man who touched you like that…who hurt you. I would kill him."

"I believe you."

"It's important that you know."

It made her want to cry. Because her parents had asked why she was bruised the next morning, but they'd also believed her lies about why. Feeble lies about tripping over her feet. They'd accepted it without batting an eye.

And when she'd started spending more and more time in her room, they just stopped asking her to come out.

Ferro made her feel like it mattered. Like she mattered.

"I really think you're a pretty good man, Ferro Calvaresi," she said.

He slid his thumb over her cheekbone, his eyes intent on hers. "I'm not, Julia. I don't want you to lie to yourself. That's just another reason we need these rules. I need to make sure you understand what this is. What this really is."

"I accept your terms," she said, an echo of the agreement she'd made with him the first time they'd made love. "But you have to agree to mine."

"And they are?"

"Don't leave me after. I want to sleep with you. I need that."

He searched her face. Unwilling to disappoint her, not now. She could read it, clearly, in his expression. "I will stay in bed with you at least until you fall asleep. I would not be able to sleep with another person."

She nodded, even though she didn't like his answer. She wouldn't push.

"Don't fake charm me. I'm not one of your clients. We might be making a deal, but we're not selling our bodies, do you understand? I want you. The real you."

"I'll give you what I can on that score, Julia, but I don't know if it will be enough for you."

"And why is that?"

"Julia, I had to work at separating my mind from my body, what I wanted, from what I needed to do. I don't just connect with people and that's not by accident. I learned something very quickly in my life. It's easy to survive if you realize you always have control of your mind. The harshest street doesn't seem so bad if you can go into yourself and imagine you have a bed, imagine you're safe. Sex with a stranger you don't even want touches your body, but you can close it out in your mind. You can go so far inside yourself that nothing touches you anymore. My problem has been finding the way back out. Honestly, I don't even want to most of the time. Except when you touch me. Then I want to feel it all."

Her heart crumpled in on itself. "I want to try to help you."

"You can help me. In my bed. I feel the most with you,

when I'm in you, that I've ever felt in my life." He reached and she extended her hand to him, let him take it, let him draw her to him. "Kiss me."

She bent down and pressed her lips to his.

"You will come home with me tonight," he said, a command, but she knew it was her choice.

She nodded, not caring that it was impractical and that she didn't have her things. Not caring about much of anything but Ferro and her need for him.

"Whatever you want."

"As per our agreement, *cara*."

And she couldn't help but feel like she'd made a deal with the devil. But she had a hard time feeling too bad about it. And the strange thing was, she didn't feel trapped anymore. Not by the media, not by her past.

She felt free.

CHAPTER TWELVE

FOR THE FOURTH night in a row, when Ferro got home after work, Julia was at his house. And for the fourth night in a row he told his chef to have dinner delivered to his room in an hour. And for the fourth night in a row, he picked Julia up and took her upstairs where he made the best use of that hour possible. Naked and beneath the covers.

Then he answered the bedroom door in his robe, closed the door, discarded it and served them both dinner in bed with nothing between them.

The past four days had been like nothing he'd ever experienced before. A woman he wanted, in his home, in his bed, answering his cravings and desires.

It was such a pleasurable arrangement it made him wish he'd put one together years ago. Except, then the woman wouldn't have been Julia. And he couldn't find it in him to be interested in the idea of having a woman other than Julia.

But that was simply because she was his lover. It was normal, he was sure, to possess a certain amount of fascination with her, to the exclusion of others. He imagined. He had never had a lover before Julia.

Her admission to him in his office, about her date, had made him feel protective of her in a way he'd never felt protective of anyone. Had made him crave violence. Had made him feel...connected. It was so very strange.

But then, the entire relationship was.

"It's a gorgeous night out." Julia climbed out of his bed and walked to the windows that overlooked the ocean. She was naked, and not at all embarrassed. He had loved watching her self-consciousness fall away. Now she seemed completely at ease with him, with or without clothes.

"It is. Do you like the stars?" He didn't know what had compelled him to ask. Why he felt compelled to share this part of himself. But he did. Because he had never shared himself with anyone. The people who had cared for him until he could care for himself were a blur. There was no love or affection from them. Only food and blankets, which, for a child on the street was enough.

Then there were his clients. Women who didn't care for him personally at all. He shared nothing of himself with them. Nothing at all.

And Julia…wonderful Julia with her excitement for life, shared her smile with him. Her happiness and joy. He wanted to share this. Something personal. Something real.

"Sci-fi geek. Love them."

"Yes, well, my love for them is not sci-fi related but, perhaps you'd like to come up to the roof and see my telescope anyway?"

Her eyebrows shot up and she looked down. "Telescope, eh? Are you trying to seduce me, Mr. Calvaresi? Because you don't have to try that hard."

He got out of bed and crossed the room to her, taking her into his arms and kissing her on the lips. "Didn't I promise not to charm you?"

"You did. But I have to confess, I'm charmed."

He wanted to tell her not to be. To warn her away. But he also wanted her to keep looking at him like that.

She went back to the bed and grabbed a blanket. "I think

this will do." She wrapped it around her shoulders and opened the door to his room. "After you."

He reached down and picked up a pair of black briefs, tugging them on before going out into the hall. "This way," he said, holding out his hand. She took it, lacing her fingers through his.

Another thing he'd never done when it wasn't for show. He just wanted to touch her. Just wanted his skin against hers.

The stairs that led to the roof curved tightly, leading up to a small garden set into the edge of the rooftop. It all overlooked the ocean and gave a brilliant view of the crystal clear sky. Out away from the city, there was no light pollution, and so many stars were visible to the naked eye, so many more than he'd imagined as a boy. The big ones, always there, helping him find his way through the dark streets, helping orient him, giving him a sense of direction.

But now, here, he could see them all. From the largest ones down to the stars that were no more than diamond dust.

He tugged her onto the white divan that was set up there, the perfect place for him to look out at all he had achieved. But that wasn't why he'd brought her here. It wasn't a show of wealth or status. He wanted to show her something of him.

"I've always been fascinated with the sky at night. I spent a lot of time looking at it when I slept out on the streets. In doorways, alleyways, wherever I could find that wasn't occupied by another homeless person. And when I had to get somewhere quickly in the dark, I used the North Star to find my way."

"You were always smart," she said, her voice soft, her fingers trailing lightly over his bare chest.

"It is what saved me. Of that I'm certain." He paused, hesitated. "When I first started making real money I got a telescope, and I started looking at the stars. It was exciting. Like meeting a friend for the first time, if that makes any sense.

But I was very alone, Julia, for most of my life. My surroundings were my only constant. My companion and my enemy."

"I can't even imagine, Ferro, but I do try."

"I know you do." It made his throat tight. What Julia did for him was more than any person had ever done.

"So show me your favorite places," she said, gesturing to the telescope.

He got up and positioned it, bending down and looking, searching. "There," he said. "The Orion nebula. I took particular joy in being able to see that. Once I got the telescope."

"New discoveries opened up to you," she said.

"Yes."

She stood up, dropped the blanket. He stepped aside and went back to the divan while she bent and looked through the telescope.

"Such a fantasy, Julia. A naked woman who takes joy in looking at the stars. I should think that's a very rare thing for a man to possess."

She straightened and looked at him. "And I have a mostly naked man who understands the sheer beauty of an eight core processor. That is also fantasy material."

"I love it when you talk nerdy to me."

She laughed and joined him on the divan, tugging the blanket up over both of them. "It's beautiful," she said.

"What is?"

"The nebula. All of it. This place. Your place. What you've done with your life, Ferro, it's not a small thing. When I first read your biography—"

"That damned book."

"I know. But when I first read it, I didn't think it could be true. Because how could a boy with no education, who had been through everything you'd been through, transcend it all and reach the place you have. You're truly amazing, and now that I see you as something other than my enemy I realize that."

"When this is over," he said, "we will still be competition. Everything is going back to how it was before. It's part of our bargain."

Something flashed through her eyes. Sadness. Deep, heartbreaking sadness. "I know. But you'll never be my enemy again, even if I'm yours."

He put his hand on her cheek, felt her skin, soft beneath his. He wanted to make her promises. Wanted to find a way to fuse the pieces of himself, as they'd been in that moment following the time they'd made love in his office. For one, brief flash of time, he had been whole, and he wanted it again so badly. So he could even begin to understand what he wanted to say. What he should say.

But he had nothing. No words. So he leaned in and kissed her, because it was what he knew. Because he knew it would cover his inadequacies.

She kissed him, sweet, giving. Giving in a way he could never hope to be.

He pushed her onto her back, kissed her neck, her collarbone, the curve of her breast. He tugged the blanket away so he could look at her body, bathed in the moonlight.

"You are without a doubt, the most beautiful thing I have seen beneath the night sky." He lowered his head, ran his tongue over her nipple and watched as it peaked in the cool outdoor air. "Without a doubt."

She put her hands on his cheeks, her eyes boring into his. "You are an amazing man, Ferro. The most amazing I have ever known. If I could make you feel what I feel. If I could give the feelings I have for you to you, I would. So you would know how incredible you are."

Her gaze, unflinching, honest, made him feel far too exposed. Made him feel like he was naked for the first time with her. Yes, he'd been naked with her many times over the course of the past week, and before that, there had been other women he'd been naked with.

Not like this. Never like this.

He lowered his head, kissed her neck, inhaled the sweet scent of her skin.

"Ferro—"

He cut her off with a kiss, moved his hand down between her thighs and started stroking her damp flesh until her words turned into sighs of pleasure. He watched her face as he pushed a finger deep inside her while stroking her clitoris with his thumb. He could do this. He could do sex. He could give her pleasure, take pleasure.

It was the talking that was causing the unbearable pressure in his chest. There could be no more talking.

"Please," she whimpered. "Please."

He pushed his underwear down his hips and positioned himself, testing her readiness, sliding into her slowly, so slowly he thought the pain of want would kill him before he was all the way home.

Then he lost himself in her. In her body, her breath fanning against his cheek, wet kisses on his neck, her nails in his shoulder blades. He lost himself in Julia and he never wanted it to end. Here with her it made sense. Life seemed to make sense. And he felt more at peace, he felt more whole, he simply felt more, than he ever had before.

Orgasm rushed over him like a wave and as she arched beneath him, crying out her release, he found his own.

When it was over, he held her against his chest, smoothed her hair. Wondered if his heart would ever slow down. If it had slowed down at all since that first night they were together.

Julia reached down and picked up the blanket, drawing it over their bodies.

"We should go in," he said.

"I don't want to," she said. "Too sleepy."

"The only alternative is sleeping out here."

"And what's wrong with that? It's a beautiful night, and we can look at the stars."

Terror expanded in his chest, pushing out the comfort and well-being he'd felt only a moment before. "I don't like being cold."

"I'll keep you warm."

"Julia," he said, sitting up. "I have not spent one night outside since I could first afford to put a roof over my head."

"But you're not back there, Ferro, it's not the same. You're not in Rome. You're not on the street. And you aren't alone." She sat up and wrapped her arms around his waist from behind, her breasts pressing into his back. "I promise I won't let you get cold."

Ferro relaxed, followed Julia's gentle tug back down to the divan. He lay on his back and looked at the stars, while Julia rested her head on his chest, her body heat seeping through his skin.

Her heat chased away the cold. The fear. And he slept.

It wasn't until he was in the office the next day that he realized what he'd done. He'd been so desperate to get Julia to stop talking, to get her to stop making him feel, to be inside her, that he'd forgotten about condoms.

That had never happened in his life. Never. Condoms were the most important thing in his sexual encounters when he'd been a prostitute. *Dio,* but he hated that word. It still had the power to flay his skin from his bones. To make him feel like less than a man.

And yet it was the truth about him. A truth he was trying to ignore, by replacing those memories with memories of Julia. He clung to her as if her touch had the power to clean all the dirt from his skin.

But far from that, he was starting to wonder if he was just spreading the dirt to her. No matter what she said. No matter what she claimed to see when she looked at him.

Actions like his didn't come clean.

I wish you could see how amazing you are.

No, she was wrong. He wasn't amazing. He was just a man selfish enough, without conscience enough, to do whatever he'd had to do to get where he wanted to go.

And now he'd brought her into it, compromised her. After all that had already happened to her...would he hurt her, too?

Damn. They had the meeting with Barrows today, too. He stood up and stalked out his office door. "No one calls me," he growled at his assistant as he walked past, contacting his driver from his phone as he did so.

He got into the elevator and took it down to the lobby where his car was already waiting, idling against the curb.

"Julia's," he said to the driver. He didn't have to say more. Everyone knew now that they were lovers. Everyone knew who Julia was.

The drive across town in the afternoon traffic was unbearable. Too hard to wait that long. He couldn't wait. When his driver was a block away, Ferro jerked open the door and got out, striding the rest of the way down the sidewalk, his focus straight ahead. He ignored the tourists, the few people who recognized him who were gaping, the sun, the palm trees that lined the walk. He ignored them all.

He walked into Julia's building and made his way up to her office.

"You can't go in there she's prepping for a mee— Oh, Mr. Calvaresi." Julia's assistant offered him a toothpaste-white smile.

"I need to see her."

"She said she didn't want to be disturbed."

"She did not mean me."

"I already got in trouble for the salmon."

"She didn't mean it. She loves it. I need to see her now. I'm going to, even if I have to break the office door down, you might as well buzz me in."

Thad smiled again and pressed a button on the desk. "Ferro Calvaresi to see you, darling."

He didn't return the other man's smile as he walked toward Julia's office doors and swung them open.

She jumped up. "Ferro." She rounded her desk and wrapped her arms around him, kissing him quickly. Such a normal, couplelike gesture. So strange to him. "I wasn't expecting you yet, we weren't supposed to meet until later."

"That is for business, this is a personal call," he said.

"Oh, really?" Her expression turned suggestive.

"No," he bit out. "Not that."

"Oh." She was hurt, and it was his fault. Because he was short with her. Much more than he'd intended to be.

"I needed to tell you, I realized that I didn't use a condom last night."

Her cheeks turned pink. "Oh."

"You're safe, in terms of your health. It's fair of you to be concerned about that all things considered. But I was very careful with my clients. And I had not had sex in twelve years, and in that time I've been tested, just in case. My concern is pregnancy, of course."

"Oh…oh that. No. No that won't be a problem."

"It won't?"

"It's a bad…time of the month and stuff."

Julia felt a little shell-shocked. A lot shell-shocked. She wasn't sure how she'd missed the oversight last night. But she had. So stupid of her. Irresponsible. And yet, shell-shocked though she was, she didn't feel terrified.

And she had no idea if she was at a fertile time in her cycle or not. She'd never really paid attention to that kind of thing since, until recently, she hadn't been sexually active. But it sounded like the right thing to say. Sounded like something she should know.

Except lying was wrong.

"I…I don't really know if it's a bad time of the month," she said. "But…but I don't want to take anything. Any pills or anything to…to stop it. I just don't want to."

He nodded slowly. "I understand."

"You do?"

"I do."

"I have enough money to take care of a baby," she said. "I could get all the help I'd need. Even if I had to bring the baby to work, I could. I'm the boss lady. There's like…no woman on earth more ready, financially speaking, to handle an accidental baby than me, and you wouldn't have to do anything."

"You think I want to do nothing?"

"You came in here all panicked."

"I don't want you to be pregnant," he said. "I don't want to raise a baby, with you or anyone else, but I'll be damned, if there is a child, if I walk away from it."

"That's…well, that's crazy."

"How? How is it crazy? Do you want to be pregnant?"

With the potential father looking at her like she was public enemy number one and all kinds of frightening unresolved feelings for the man? No. No she did not.

"No."

"But if you were pregnant?"

"I would love my baby. I would take care of it."

"So then, I'm not crazy."

"Look, nice cart, but the horse doesn't go behind it."

"What?"

"Cart before the horse. I'm probably not pregnant. Let's all chill."

"This kind of a lapse is unacceptable, Julia."

"Okay, so let's be more responsible then."

"It never should have happened."

Julia felt her ears starting to burn. "Great. Fine. So it won't happen again. We'll be more careful."

"Because…"

"Stop it!" she shouted. "Stop reiterating how awful it would be to have a child with me, please. I can't take the repeated statements of your horror."

"Don't make this about your insecurities, Julia, it's bigger than that."

"I'm sorry, it's hard not to make it about my insecurities since…you know it's so heavily about me."

"And about a child," he said, his words clipped. "Do you really think I should raise a child? Do you think I'm daddy material? What life lessons do I have to pass on? If you're struggling, don't give up, sell yourself to the highest bidder?"

"But you wouldn't let our child struggle," she said, her voice muted.

"But I would still be who I am." He looked out the window, past her. "It is, in some ways, a blessing I have no family. No one who loves me. Because they would be horrified by the man I had to become to get to the place I'm standing in now. I know I am. I'll see you in a couple of hours, at Barrows. Be ready to make the presentation of a lifetime."

She nodded slowly and watched him walk out of her office. Something in her chest burned. Fought for recognition, fought to get through all the walls she'd built up, to tear off the blinders she'd put on. It burned until it hurt. Until the words swam through her head, clear and undeniable.

That's where you're wrong, Ferro. Someone does love you.

She put her hand on her stomach and hoped the wave of nausea would pass. Yeah, she'd done something really stupid. She'd fallen for her first. She'd fallen for Ferro. Their relationship had brought her through so much, had taught her so much about herself. It had helped her strip off her armor, and find she didn't need it anymore.

And she'd started, not just to love him, but to trust him.

But she hadn't done that for him. He was still the same. Still at the point he'd been when they'd first began.

And no matter what sort of lie she'd told herself to the contrary, sleeping under the stars with him hadn't meant a damn thing.

Except it had to her. It had meant everything.

This deal is what's supposed to mean everything. Barrows is supposed to mean everything.

Yeah, it was. But all she could think of was that when this presentation was over, when the deal was made, there would be no real reason for Ferro to share her bed anymore.

And that was something she simply wasn't ready to think about.

CHAPTER THIRTEEN

JULIA WAS SO filled with energy she had to jiggle her knee beneath the table to keep it from spilling over completely.

"Don't be nervous," Ferro said.

"I'm not. Just excited. Everyone will be here soon and we get to pitch out an idea and it is so awesome."

"Hamlin will be here, too."

"He's pitching in the same meeting? Oh. Goody."

"Not my preference, either. I was only told in my last phone call with Weston just before I got here."

"At least the CEO called you. He didn't call me."

"I'm the lead on the project," he said, his smile reflecting that easy charm of his. But this time, the teasing seemed genuine.

"Like hell, billionaire man, this is just as much mine as yours." She reached under the table and grabbed his hand, squeezing him gently. He froze and pulled away.

She was about to say something when the door opened and the board of directors for Barrows, plus all the executives and Scott Hamlin, filed into the room.

Hamlin was clearly taking the "suck-up" approach to the whole thing. His hand was glued to Carl Weston's back, his laugh too loud and too obvious as they made their way to their seats.

Introductions were made, and Scott got up to give the first

presentation. Julia's confidence and all around smugness increased the longer Hamlin talked about his product. It was nowhere near as sophisticated as theirs. Nowhere near as user friendly or generally awesome.

She had almost tuned him out, his speech was so boring, when he came to the wrap-up.

"In short, I think you'll find my product to be exactly to the briefing. Inexpensive to manufacture and easy to repair should something go wrong, not that it will. And even more importantly, my company will not put a stain on the reputation of Barrows. At Hamlin Tech we uphold family values. Unlike the sort of values my opponents seem to uphold, or rather denigrate. But then, let's be honest, we know Mr. Calvaresi is a professional at seducing what he wants out of a woman. And unlike Ms. Anderson, no one at Hamlin has ever sold their body to the competition to get ahead." He leveled his gaze at Julia when he said the last bit, and it stung. Like a whip across her skin. She knew it wasn't true, that she'd had Ferro because she wanted him and for no other reason. The irony was him accusing *her* of selling her body, when it was much closer to Ferro's truth. But he was just the sort of man who would assume that about a woman, the sort of man who had no respect for women at all. Just another reason to grind him into the dirt with their awesome presentation.

The room was deadly silent when he sat down and Julia waited for someone, anyone to reprimand him. But no one did. She looked at Ferro and the glint in his eye could only be described as deadly.

She leaned in. "Let's just make the presentation. He doesn't matter. It doesn't matter."

They stood and she started saying her part, that she'd thankfully rehearsed enough that she only needed a quarter of her brainpower to focus on it. The rest could quietly panic and simmer in humiliation over what had just happened.

Then it was Ferro's turn to talk about the technical specifications and he did, quickly, his voice getting rougher as he spoke until he turned to Scott Hamlin. "I'm not certain what sort of family values you ascribe to," he said, addressing the man directly, making no effort to veil where he was directing his words. "But as far as I know, the sexual harassment of employees is not a family value. Furthermore, I don't care what you think of me. I am everything they say and so much worse. What I had to do to survive on the streets is one long, ugly story, and it is my story. But if you dare to ever imply that Julia has somehow gotten to the position she's in by any means other than hard work and her sheer brilliance, I will show you some other survival tricks I learned on the streets. And I can guarantee you won't just walk away from that demonstration."

The room had reached a new level of quiet. Julia could only stare, her face hot. With anger, with humiliation and with adrenaline. She was proud of Ferro. She wanted to kill Ferro. She couldn't believe what had just happened.

He took her arm and started to lead her from the room. "Ferro…"

"Call us with your decision," Ferro tossed over his shoulder as they walked out of the boardroom and into the hall.

"Ferro! You just…you probably just killed that deal for us."

"They should not have let him say that," Ferro spat, releasing his hold on her and walking ahead to the elevator. "They should not have let him say such things about you. Someone should have spoken up."

"In fairness, it might look like I…with you…to get this…"

"Why should you need to? I need you just as much as you need me in this. To imply otherwise is insulting to you as a person and a businesswoman and I will not allow it."

The elevator doors closed and Julia leaned against the wall, suddenly feeling very tired. "I've been insulted more than once in my life, Ferro," she said "It's why I don't go around being all happy-happy joy-joy Julia all the time. It's why I don't talk about spaceships and games and my new processor in polite company. I can honestly say, though, that I've never been accused of using my body to get what I want. I suppose that's what I get for having a sex life."

"It's wrong."

"But I'm fine. I would have been fine if you would have just kept your mouth shut and made the presentation."

He turned to her, dark eyes blazing. "But I wouldn't have been." He pushed the button on his phone she knew now called his driver.

The elevator doors slid open and Ferro's breathing started to normalize, the color draining slightly from his face. As if he'd just realized what he had done. They walked through the glass and steel building, out onto the warm, sunny street.

"Perhaps you should stay at your own house tonight, Julia," he said.

She nodded slowly. "Okay. I mean…if you really want me to." She wanted to ask him to change his mind. Wanted to tell him she needed to be with him after a day like today. No one else would understand. But he would, not just because he'd been there, but because it was his life, too. His passion.

She wanted to sit on the couch with him and drink a glass of wine and talk about how horrible the whole thing had been. And then she wanted to spend all night making love with him.

But he wanted her to go home.

"I guess I'll…" And she realized they didn't have a reason to see each other again. "I guess I'll see you," she said. She hoped it was true.

He nodded once and walked to his car. Julia stuck her hand in her pocket and took out her phone, getting ready to dial her driver. She really should get Ferro's stupid app because she didn't want to talk to her driver, she wanted to call for him nonverbally so she didn't have to say a word past the ache in her throat.

She decided to text him, even though that wasn't a normal way for her to communicate with him. But it worked. He pulled up five minutes after Ferro had already left.

"Mr. Calvaresi's house?" he asked.

Her stomach tightened, stealing her breath. Oh, yes, because that's where she'd gone every night over the course of the past week.

"No. My house. Thanks."

"Did the presentation go well, Ms. Anderson?"

"No," she said, leaning her head against the seat. "It did not go well."

In the end, she decided to do a big blanket, sweats and a glass of wine on her own. She didn't need Ferro to sulk with. She could sulk all by herself. And if it was a little lonely, a little cold and a whole lot sadder, then fine. She could deal. She was sulking after all.

She picked up her remote from the couch and hit the stereo button, then pressed Play. A little smooth jazz would make a nice soundtrack to her hard times.

She was a billionaire. She should totally blow off sulking over a man and fly to Paris to sample wine and cheese or something.

No, she wasn't sulking over a man, though. She was sulking over the presentation. The presentation was the important thing. It was why she'd agreed to the Ferro ruse in the first place.

Ugh. Then why didn't she care more?

She set her wine on the table beside the couch and drew her knees up to her chest. An alarm pinged, the sound of a vehicle at her gate, and she sat up straight, grabbing the remote again and aiming it at the TV, turning on the security feed.

It was a dark sports car, but she couldn't see the driver. She hit the intercom button. "Can I help you?"

"I hope you can."

The sound of Ferro's voice made her heart jump up into her throat.

"I hope I can, too. Come up." She pushed the button that released the lock on the gate and sat back down on the couch, wringing her hands. What was she doing? Why had she told him he could come up? She should be all mad at him.

Except she still wanted to be with him. Even when she was mad.

She jumped up from the couch and downed the last of her wine, then looked down at her sweats. *"Mmf."* They weren't exactly what she wanted him to see her in. But then, the other option was stripping down to her undies or further really quick and she wasn't sure he was here for that.

Anyway, he'd seen her in sweats before. Just not so much since they'd become full-time lovers.

Then he was knocking on the door, heavily, and she didn't have time to waffle. She set her glass down and went to the door, bent on owning the sweats look now.

She pulled the door open and stood there, her hand on her hip. "What brings you here?"

Ferro looked down at Julia, her curves concealed by her baggy sweats, and he nearly sank to the floor in relief. Just the sight of her did so much to him. Just the thought of her was enough to keep him awake, to drive him from his bed in the middle of the night so he could see her. So he could be near her.

"I could not sleep," he said, walking in past her.

"Come in."

Ferro set his computer bag down on the floor and started toward her living room.

Much like their offices. Hers was what she'd thought an

important businesswoman might have in her house. Neutrals, large windows that overlooked the sea. Beige and lots of it, with little pops of lime and blue here and there. Sedate and expensive.

It was starkly different to his house, his office. Which was what he'd imagined someone with money should have. Everything he owned was a testament to disposable income, while Julia's was so much more…normal than she was. Normal and boring. Nothing like her. But it would show the world that she was more like them. Would make her look like less of a bubbly, eccentric genius.

It was a shame. A shame that anything, any man, anyone, had made her hide herself. He wanted to tell her but the words stuck in his throat.

She put her hands on her hips. "Are you blaming me for your lack of sleep, or just coming to share the misery?"

"I am blaming you," he said, anger so much easier to find than sincerity. "I have never had a problem dealing with sexual frustration, and trust me, Julia, twelve years of celibacy means I had my share."

Her eyes rounded. "I just assumed you didn't want sex in all that time."

"I didn't want the baggage. The reminder. I missed the orgasms. But it's not a matter of a cold shower or taking care of things on my own, not now. Not when all I can think of is what's missing." The words were broken, scraped his throat raw on the way out. "The way you feel, the way you smell. The way you touch me. You have ruined things for me."

"Oh, gee, well, thanks."

"I want you. Now." Need. It was so much more than want. It was need.

"I…" For a moment, just a moment, she looked like she might say no, and he couldn't bear it. He was shaking inside, with need, with…he didn't even know what.

"On our original terms," he said. "I give the orders, and you say yes."

Control would help. Control was what he needed. A way to make this all make sense. A way to make it something he recognized. Something he could deal with.

Julia looked into Ferro's eyes, black, haunted, endless. A man who was wounded, hunted. She could see it. Feel the desperation. He was demanding control because it was the only thing holding him together.

Because it was the only way he could handle things between them.

"Yes," she said. An agreement she shouldn't make, but one she needed just as badly as he did.

"Take your top off," he said.

"Here?" she asked, looking out the windows at the beach. It was a private beach, but even so.

"Modesty from the woman who went stargazing on my roof naked?"

Yes, but that had been different. A moment of connection and sweetness rather than this...intensity that was arcing between them.

"This was not a request, Julia, it was an order. Take off your top, or I am going to leave."

She caught an even more revealing glimpse then. Of his frayed control. Of the reason behind the orders. And it hit her then that for all his dominant manner, Ferro wasn't the one in control of this moment. She grabbed the hem of her sweater and pulled it up over her head.

He looked at her breasts, covered by a black bra, and smiled. This wasn't a light, charming smile. This one was dark. Wicked. Perfect.

"Now your pants."

She obeyed this time without needing prompting, pushing

her sweatpants down her legs and kicking them to the side, the game, the intensity, arousing her past the point of reason.

"Now," he said, "I want you to go upstairs. Walk ahead of me. Don't turn around."

She sucked in a breath and turned away from him, walked toward the curved staircase. She felt completely on display. The stairs were open all the way up to the second floor, making the most of the view. But now, she had the feeling she was the view.

She felt powerful, and vulnerable, weak and strong, at the same time. But then, being with Ferro had that effect on her. With him she felt more secure than she ever had, and more terrified of where her life was heading than she ever had. Happier with what she had, more afraid of the potential loss.

Loss was the only place this could end.

She swallowed hard and kept walking, the marble floor cold beneath her feet, and Ferro's steps hard and purposeful behind her.

She opened her bedroom door and paused, waiting for her next order, her heart pounding in her ears.

"Get on the bed," he said. "Look straight ahead."

She walked to the bed and got on it, as instructed.

"Go to the center, on your knees."

She obeyed again, her hands trembling as she did. She heard his footsteps behind her, felt the mattress depress as he got on the bed.

She felt the hot press of his mouth in the center of her shoulder blades and she shivered, pleasure streaking through her like a lightning bolt. She started to turn.

"No," he said. "Look ahead."

She took a breath and tried to keep her gaze focused on the curtains in front of her.

"Do these open by remote?"

She nodded.

"Where?" he asked.

"Over there." She indicated a button by the nightstand, and Ferro pressed it. The curtains parted to reveal the ocean, the moon glimmering on the surface of the waves.

"There," he said, "now you have a view to keep you occupied."

He pressed a kiss to her shoulder, then replaced his lips with his finger, tracing a line down the center of her back, ending just above the waistband of her panties.

She felt like she was going to die of the slow, erotic torture he was wreaking on her.

"You have a beautiful back, Julia. The first time I felt attraction for you was at the movie premiere, when you had all this skin on display. I didn't recognize my feelings for what they were. I'd spent too many years ignoring them to identify them easily. But that's what it was. And it was partly due to this gorgeous back."

He ran the tip of his finger between her shoulder blades.

Then he reached down and undid the clasp of her bra. It fell forward and down her arms, she took it off the rest of the way, pushing it aside.

He reached around and cupped her breasts, teased her nipples until she was breathing hard. Until she couldn't think. She kept her eyes fixed on the moon, kept herself from turning around and kissing him.

"Perfect," he said. "You are so perfect. Now I want you to grab on to your headboard, can you do that for me?"

"Yes."

She obeyed his command, her heart beating harder now. She wanted to look at him. Wanted to touch him. Wanted to connect with him. This was great, it felt great, but she wanted to see him. Wanted to try to read his emotions. And he wasn't allowing it.

Then she forgot to be bothered, because as she took ahold

of the headboard, he started to tug her panties down, leaving them on just above her knees. Then he gripped her hips and pulled her toward him, pressed an intimate kiss to her damp flesh, slid his tongue through her folds.

Then he straightened, pushing a finger inside her. "Ready for me?" he asked.

"Yes."

"Good." She could hear him tearing open a condom packet, could hear him undoing the buckle on his belt and a pause while she assumed he was applying the protection.

Then he was pushing inside her, impossibly deep, filling her to the point of discomfort for a moment, before her body acclimated and pain gave way to pleasure.

"Good?" he asked, his voice rough, his movements slow.

The only response she had was a deep moan as she lowered her head and held on to the bed for all she was worth.

He thrust into her hard, one hand braced just beneath her breasts, the other on her hip, as he found his rhythm. She could feel the moment his control started to shred, when each thrust brought a short groan from his lips, his movements becoming more desperate, harder, faster.

Finally she had to look. Had to touch. Had to taste. She turned and captured his mouth with hers.

When she broke the kiss, she looked at his eyes, blank, bleak. A man haunted. A man possessed. He moved his hand to cup her breast, shifted the other one so that it was between her thighs, stroking the source of her pleasure.

And then that was all she could feel. All she could think about. The release that was building in her, drawing her body so tight she was sure it would break her.

But just as she reached her limit, its hold broke, the tension unraveling, sending her into a free fall as endless waves crashed over her, flooded through her. He moved his hands to her hips, stiffening behind her, a harsh growl signaling his own release.

He lay down, bringing her with him, keeping her so that her back was to him. He held her close, saying nothing, his heart pounding heavily, so much so she could feel it echoing in her own body.

He was still dressed. His shirt was scratchy on her back, his belt buckled digging into her butt. "Could you scoot?" she asked. "Or, why don't you just take your clothes off."

She turned over and kissed him, but he didn't kiss her back. "Ferro?"

He sat up and she thought maybe he was going to get undressed. But then he stood and removed the condom, redoing his belt buckle on his way into her bathroom to dispose of the protection.

"What are you doing?" she asked.

"I'm leaving."

Panic clawed at her, and she tried to calm it down. Because it was useless to get all worked up. Useless to show her pain and her worry over such a simple statement. Except she felt the deeper meaning in it. What he was really saying.

Still, she tried to ignore it. Tried to play it down.

"If you're worried about not having a toothbrush, you can use mine. And before you say gross, I'm pretty sure we've swapped enough germs to…"

She trailed off when she looked at his expression. At his eyes. So detached. Unfocused. He wasn't even looking at her.

"Ferro, don't do this," she said.

"Don't do what, Julia?"

"You know what you're doing, don't pretend. You're trying to put distance between us, that's what all of this has been about. All of tonight."

"I don't have to try to put distance between us. That's all

there has ever been between us. Our bodies have been close, we have not been."

"That's not true. It's not."

"It is. I'm sorry if that's a hard truth for you, Julia, but it is."

"You are such a coward!" she said, screamed, really, because she couldn't believe what he was doing. Couldn't believe that he was standing there in slacks and a button up shirt, perfectly pressed still, ready to walk out the door like nothing had happened, while she was naked and rumpled and completely altered by what had happened between them.

"A coward, Julia? Is that what you think? You attribute far too much emotion to me, *cara mia*."

"You hide so well, Ferro, you even manage to hide from yourself. But you can't hide from me. I know you."

"You think you know me because I told you some stories about my past? Because we slept together?"

"No, I think I know you because I understand how those things made you feel. I understand that you don't feel all blasé and whatever about your past. I know that it hurts. I know you won't let yourself move on because you feel dirty. Because you're so scared. Of what, I don't know. But you cling to your past like you need it to protect you. To remind you."

"Look at you pretending you have it all figured out. You're hiding, too, Julia."

"I was. You're right. But…I'm not going to now. I can't now. I was so afraid to ever trust. How could I trust anyone? Ever. How could I show I was vulnerable? Look what happened to me when I tried. My mother, my own mother, chose a date for me who tried to rape me. Of course I had trouble with it. Of course I hid. But you made me see how great it was to just come out and be me. I trust you. With everything. Everything I have, everything I am. I love you, Ferro. We both deserve more than we've given ourselves. Who cares what anyone else thinks? Who cares about the past? We have a present. We have a future, why should the past get all the play?"

"You don't love me, Julia. You're just a girl who got introduced to sex and thinks an orgasm is the same as feelings."

The barb hit its mark, sinking in deep, the pain in her chest radiating outward. Again, she'd shown herself, all of herself, to someone, and again she had been rejected.

"You don't get to tell me what I feel," she said, anger propelling her forward rather than letting her hide. "I love you."

"Dammit, woman, where is your sense of self-preservation? You were better off with your armor than you are showing off all your emotion for the world to see. To use against you. Do you know how easily crushed you are?"

Julia sucked in a breath. "Does my emotion frighten you?" she asked. He said nothing so she pressed on. "I'm sorry my passion and enthusiasm and human emotion make you uncomfortable, Ferro. I am." She paused, focused on what she felt, on all the emotion that was coursing through her. And she realized how much she'd held back, for so long, in order to please others. She was done with that. Starting now.

"No, you know what? I'm not sorry. I'm done apologizing for being me. I'm done feeling bad for being who I am. I'm a geek. And I laugh too loud, because when I think something is funny, I think it's really funny. If I like a game or a movie, I really like it. Like, dress up in costume like it. I will never fit in. I will never be normal. And when I love someone…I love with everything. With all of me. Ferro, I love you. If that bothers you, fine. But I'm not going to stop. I'm not going to sublimate it, or play it cool. I'm going to shout it, and *feel* it, breathe it, live it, and no one is going to tell me I can't, or it's wrong, or it's embarrassing. Yeah, I'm through apologizing. I'm done hiding. I love you. I'm not sorry. So it's your move now. You have to tell me no if that's what you want, but you can't pretend that I don't know my mind, that this is somehow not real. If you're going to reject me, you have to face what it is you're rejecting."

When she finished, she was breathing hard, but she felt more alive, more her, than she had for years. If Ferro was going to reject her, he had to reject her. Not some polished version of herself she'd created to seem more powerful, more capable. But the version of herself he'd brought back to the surface.

The girl who had had unreserved enjoyment in life, who had cared about everything, from games to prom, so much. The girl she'd stuffed down and hidden to avoid getting hurt. Well, now she was standing with everything out in the open, vulnerable, easily destroyed. But she had to do it. For him. For them.

"This has been an enjoyable arrangement for me," he said, his voice monotone. "I hate to see it end. However, it's clear to me that it must."

She wanted to scream at him. She bit her lip, a tear falling down her cheek. He was hiding. Hiding still. Behind a mask. Behind his scars.

"You know we can't really go back," she said. "We'll never go back to how things were. We were stupid, Ferro. We thought we would control it, but it controlled us."

"I'll go back," he said, his voice hard. "Like it never happened, *cara*. Because that's what I do. Sex is nothing to me. Nothing."

"You don't mean that. Not with me."

"As you've been such a good lover, I would like to increase your payment." Another tear fell and she shook her head, begging him, internally, not to do this. But he continued. He bent down and picked up the computer bag he'd brought with him, pulled out a folder. "Everything I have collected on your company over the past five years. Some of it I haven't even looked at yet. It was for use at a later date. After our peaceable term ended. But I'm giving it to you. With the promise that I will never make an attempt at bringing Anfalas down. You're safe from me."

He extended the folder to her, as if he expected her to take it and thank him for it.

"I don't want it," she said.

"That's not how this works, Julia. You gave me sex, I'm giving you payment."

"I gave you my damn soul, Ferro. You can't buy that."

"But I didn't ask for your soul, my dear." His special endearment for her, in English for the first time. "I only asked for your body, so it is all I will pay for."

"You have to cheapen it, don't you? Not so you'll understand it, but so you can put it with the rest of the things in your life you're ashamed of. Because you like shame, don't you? It keeps you insulated. Keeps you from having to move on. Protects you from your feelings."

"I don't have feelings, Julia. Not for you. Not for anyone."

"Tell me you don't love me," she said, because she was perverse, because she had to hear it. "Tell me, and I'll take your 'payment' and I'll let you go."

"I don't love you."

Another tear rolled down her cheek. "Great. Then it's really over." She bent down and took the folder from the bed, held it over her bare breasts, needing cover now. Ashamed of her nudity. She wiped a tear from her cheek and lifted her hand, treating him to her best Vulcan salute. "Live long and prosper. And get the hell out of my house."

Ferro nodded once and then turned around, walking out of her room, closing the door firmly behind him. Julia sank onto the bed, her legs trembling, her stomach threatening to rebel and release its contents.

She swallowed hard. Then she lay down, still holding the folder tight against her chest, and cried.

* * *

Ferro stormed out of Julia's house and to his car, the engine roaring to life with the push of a button on his phone.

It was done. What he'd needed to do was done.

He couldn't stay with her. Couldn't indulge himself any longer. The woman was too destructive to him. She was too adept at reaching inside him and making him feel things. It was like she was hot-wiring his soul, reconnecting wires that had long ago been cut. Sending jolts of emotion and need and pain through him.

And what it had done to his control was unacceptable. Unprotected sex first, and then his outburst in the meeting. And tonight he'd come to prove that he still had the power in the relationship. That he was in charge. That he was not at the mercy of one skinny blonde who should, by all rights, drive him completely insane.

But when she'd kissed him, kissed him with all her heart, emotion pouring from her, forcing him to feel, he'd known he had lost. And so he'd deferred to his backup plan.

Draw a line beneath the relationship. Make it a transaction, like every sexual encounter that had come before. Make it so she wasn't different. So she wasn't essential.

And she had cried. Every tear a drop of acid inside him, burning away the scars, the protection.

He felt like hell. He had betrayed her, like so many other people in her life. He had let her down. He had hurt her.

He had never hated himself more. Not even as he'd stripped down for women he didn't even want and followed their every command. Not even then.

He got into his car and threw it in Drive, going too fast down the winding driveway that led out to the main highway. He needed to forget. Needed to figure out how to pull emotion from his chest as he'd once done.

To once again separate his desires from his needs. His mind from his body.

But the scent of Julia was on his clothes. His skin. He had a feeling it went down deeper than that. That she had a mark on him, in him, that would not be so easily removed.

The need to do that wasn't about preserving his business. Wasn't about preventing outbursts in meetings and undoubtedly costing himself major accounts.

It was just about survival.

He had to find a way to survive.

Suddenly the pain in his chest was so blinding he had to pull his car off the road. He sat and waited, trying to breathe, waiting for the feeling of loss, the feeling of emptiness to pass.

But it didn't. It just kept crashing over him, wave after relentless wave, and with it, images of Julia. Julia, excited about a project. Julia, rambling about a game. Julia, as she looked when they made love. Julia, crying.

It took him a moment to realize his cheeks were wet, too, like the Julia in his mind's eye.

He couldn't remember the last time emotion had had so much control over him, the last time the pieces of himself had felt so united, all of them crying out in pain over the loss of her.

And it was his own fault. He had pushed her away. Because he had been afraid of this. This pain, this loss of his protection. When everything was fragmented, it was easy enough to deal with it all. Emotion went to its own place to be dealt with later, as did the needs of his body.

But since Julia it was all out of his hands, a jumbled up mess inside him.

Just like it was for normal, everyday people.

So this was what it was like to be normal. This was what it was to feel. He hit the steering wheel, hoping the pain on his hand would deaden the pain in his chest.

It didn't work.

She was right about him. He was a coward. Clinging to the past to protect himself against anything that might happen in the future.

But she'd taken the choice from him. He was stripped bare. Too late for protection, too late to keep himself from feeling.

He would find it again. He had to. He would find a way to rebuild the walls that had been around his heart. He just needed time away from Julia.

And then things could go back to the way they'd been before she walked into his life. All he had to do was forget.

CHAPTER FOURTEEN

EVERYTHING IN HIS house was hideous. Ugly and gaudy, a testament to money. Money that meant absolutely nothing when the house was empty of everything but horrible artwork. He'd been trying to forget for five days. It was two in the morning and he was well on his way to being drunk, but he still hadn't forgotten.

She haunted him. His bed was cold. His heart was cold. It was a cold that ran deep. No night on the street had ever felt so bad. No stripping of his pride in the bed of a woman he despised had ever left him feeling quite so sick.

Losing Julia showed everything he'd built up in his life for the false facade it was.

He had not changed. He was still a scared boy with nothing and no one at the end of the day. Money hadn't changed that. And it wouldn't.

The only thing that could change was him. Even thinking about it scared him. Because if he opened himself up, he might remember. Might have to deal with the full force of his feelings, feelings from the past twelve years that he'd blunted. He'd blocked it all out to avoid the pain.

But without it, he would never have her. Without emotion, he could never have joy.

He looked around. At all the ugly, bloody artwork on his walls. On pedestals. Such opulent, pristine surroundings that meant less than nothing. He hated it all. What it represented. The type of man it proved him to be. He'd sold his soul for marble and plaster, for canvas and paint. For money. And now he was empty inside, while his house and bank account were full.

A damned sorry trade.

He walked over to a pedestal with a bust of an emperor on it and looked the thing in its white, hollow eyes. Eyes that probably had more substance than his own. Then he pushed it over, watched it shatter like dust on the floor. And he did the same to the vase beside it.

Meaningless. All of it. Without her, what did it mean?

He went down to one knee, the pain in his chest crippling. Ferro lowered his head and pressed his palms against his eyes. He felt it all crash in. The darkness, the shame. The hatred. For himself. For the women who'd used him. He felt like he was sinking in the mud, shrouded in darkness.

But in his mind there was one spot of brightness. One bit of sunshine.

It was Julia. She was reaching her hand down to him, offering to pull him out. Offering to free him. And he had turned her away.

Damn him to hell, he had turned away his salvation.

Julia exited the bathroom adjacent to her office and put her head down on her desk. The cramps she'd been dealing with all day had now been explained by the timely arrival of her period. Which was great, because it meant she wasn't pregnant. But she honestly didn't feel like throwing a party about it.

It just confirmed that her relationship with Ferro was going to be over, well and truly over, soon. There would be no link between them. No evidence of their time spent together.

Except maybe their GPS for Barrows. If that deal went

through, then they would have that. But she really wasn't holding her breath on that score. Not right now.

No. That wasn't true. She wasn't going to let there be nothing. She lifted her head and punched the intercom that connected her with Thad's desk.

"Thad? Order one of those big, obnoxious life-size soldiers from *Cold Planet*."

"A real one or one from a novelty store?"

"The novelty store will do just fine," she said, cutting him off. She was going to put it in her living room. Because she liked that stuff, and she didn't let herself have it. Because it was weird and geeky and she'd been trying so hard not to be. Because it revealed too much of her unsophisticated self. Of her real self. The self that had been battered, taken advantage of. Ridiculed.

But Ferro had shown her that she didn't need to hide. That she didn't need to be scared.

That it didn't matter what anyone else thought of her, because who she was mattered. She was successful because of her focused nature. Because of her enthusiasm. She'd surged ahead of the pack and made success for herself, not in spite of those things about her that had made it hard to make friends, that had made her parents think she was weird, but because of them.

Ferro had helped her see that. He'd helped her reconcile the pain from her past. Helped her put it all where it belonged. She'd thought she'd been over it, because she'd felt strong, but it had been a lie. And she'd gone into hiding, afraid that if she was ever pulled from her cocoon again, she would be hurt again.

And she had been. But she wouldn't hide. Not again.

She would always be thankful to him for that. Not so much for the salmon that was still in her office, or for the broken heart that still, a week later, hurt like hell.

Her intercom buzzed and Thad's voice filled the office again. "Julia, he's on his way in…"

Julia looked up just as Ferro walked into her office.

"What are you doing here?" she asked.

He had a beard. She'd never seen him with a beard. But it looked like he hadn't bothered to shave at all in the past six days.

"I've had news from Barrows."

"And?"

"They gave the account to Hamlin."

"Oh." She honestly couldn't believe it. Even with Ferro's display of macho anger, she'd felt like Hamlin had behaved even worse, and his GPS had been inferior. "I can't even believe they picked him after that cheap family values shot. He's so transparent and…"

"I threatened the man's life in front of them, our odds weren't good."

"Our GPS was better," she said, feeling stubborn now. "And I'm not pregnant. I thought I'd throw that in there real quick since we're getting to end our association now. Really and completely."

"You aren't pregnant?" he asked, his expression strange, veiled.

"Nope. Not gestating the heir to your techie empire. Sorry."

"Julia…"

"And I still can't believe they picked Hamlin! We won that. We *won it*. Ours was so much better."

"It doesn't matter, they picked him." He started pacing the length of the office. "This is your fault, you know?"

"My fault? How is this my fault? You're the one who lost your cookies in the meeting, in front of everyone!"

"Because he insulted you," Ferro said. "And I could not stop myself. I lost all of my control, and that has never happened to me, not since I learned the importance of it. It's you.

You're the only thing that's different. You have changed me. And I cannot, for the life of me figure out how to change back. Six days, Julia, six days and I can't eat. I can think of nothing but you. I feel like my heart has left my chest and is walking around outside of it. Do you know how terrifying that feeling is?"

"Yes," she said, "I do because that's how I feel. Like my heart is walking around outside my body and you, you're my heart. When you walked away you took that away from me and I…and everything just sucks! I don't care about the GPS. I don't care about the deal at all, and it's the whole reason we got together in the first place. But I don't even want it anymore, Ferro, I just want you."

He strode to her desk and rounded it, reaching for her hands and tugging her up into his arms, kissing her, bold, deep, fierce. And when she pulled back and looked into his eyes, she saw him unveiled. Truly. Finally.

Emotion blazed from him, passion. And there was no control. He kissed with everything he'd held back from her for the past few weeks. She had a feeling it was everything he'd held back for the past thirty-four years of his life.

When they parted, neither of them could catch their breath. He brushed his thumb over her cheek, wiped her tears away. Tears she hadn't realized were falling.

"You were right about me," he said. "I was a coward. I learned early on in life that the more you need, the more you can have taken. The more you care, the more power you give to other people. I had to force myself to stop feeling when I made the choices I did. I had to stop so I could get through it, and when it was over I was afraid if I started feeling again I would have to face the full horror of who I had become in order to get ahead in life."

"You make it sound like you did it on a whim. Ferro, you were saving your life. You were doing it for food. For shelter.

For things I had given to me, things I've taken for granted all my life."

"I know," he said. "But it didn't change the fact that it... broke something in me. The way I saw sex. The way I saw relationships. Not just that I had a hard time connecting sex and emotion, but that it seemed an impossibility. I had worked so hard to separate my body from my own desires, from my emotions, that I didn't think I could ever unite them again. And I didn't want to. Because it would hurt too much. Cost too much. But I faced it, Julia. I did. I looked down into the darkest parts of myself and I saw the pain. The destruction."

He kissed the corner of her mouth. "And then there was you. I thought I could give in to my body's desire for you and keep my emotions separate. After all, I had done it with women I didn't want. How hard could it be to take what I wanted for a while and walk away? But I didn't count on you. You and your joy. Your innocence. Your enthusiasm. You are everything that I had beaten out of me. You bring it back to me. Show me a part of life that I have never gotten to have and I want to hold on to it, to you, forever."

"You... Ferro you make me proud of who I am. You make me feel like I'm special. Except...except when you left. That hurt me. It broke my heart."

"It broke mine, Julia, and I didn't even know I had a heart left in me to break. A shocking discovery. Even more shocking is the fact that you make me want to feel. I thought...I thought I would get to a certain position in life and nothing would touch me. Nothing would hurt. There would be no more shame or fear, but it was always there. Money, things, didn't fix it. I was to the point where I was a man with billions of dollars, afraid to sleep outside because it might make me cold. Because it might take me back to the places I'd been. But, Julia, you make me not so afraid, you and the feelings I have for you. The answer has never been in money, it's never been in status. Those things didn't change me."

"Any more than my clothes changed me," she said.

"No. What changed me was you. Loving you. You put the pieces of me back together. You made me whole. And if you can take me…a man who has been where I've been, done what I've done, if you can take me and love me, then I really can let it go. If you can forgive it, I can, too."

She kissed him, hard, with everything she had. "There is nothing to forgive. Nothing in your life makes me feel ashamed of you. I am proud. Proud to know you. Proud to love you. Because of you I'm even proud of me."

"I love you, Julia. I have never felt this emotion before. I've never said those words before."

"I am honored to be your first lover. Your first love," she said. "Oh, and I have something for you." She reached down into her desk drawer and pulled out a folder, the folder he'd given her, and handed it to him. "For you. To do whatever you see fit with."

He turned around and put the file through her industrial shredder. Then turned back to her. "How's that?"

"I hope you aren't still planning on not taking me down simply because you're attempting to pay me back."

"No. But I'm not ever going to try to take Anfalas down because you fill a space Datasphere doesn't. The world needs you. Needs your creativity. Your passion. Just like I do."

"Now that's the nicest thing anyone has ever said to me."

"You deserved to hear it much sooner."

"I'm fine with the fact that I heard it first now. That I heard it from you. You're the first person who's made me feel like being me was enough. The first person who's ever made me feel like nothing was wrong with me."

"Your parents…that boy at your school…they wanted you to be a garden variety flower, Julia. To put you in your place.

Something they could understand and manipulate with ease. But you are something much more beautiful, much more rare. That they couldn't see, and that is a commentary on their vision, not on you. They were threatened by you because you're a force, a beauty that can't be contained. It is…a crime that those people stole your color. That they made you feel you had to hide it. I believe you were made to shine."

"See, you say things like that and…and I believe them."

"I'm so glad you do. Perhaps we can't make each other see exactly what we see in each other. But we can keep saying it."

"I have no problem with that." Julia looked down at the shredder, where the file with all the ill-gotten information about Anfalas had gone. "Hey, Ferro…how would you like to do a little partnering?"

"On what?"

"Have you ever thought of expanding in to the auto industry?"

"The auto industry?"

"Our kick-butt GPS needs some cars to go into. Seems like it might be a pretty cool adventure. And the JulErro page has like…fifty thousand likes at this point, so it seems to me like we could really get some easy buzz going."

Julia was off and running with her idea and Ferro could only watch in awe as she explained, with grand hand gestures and glittering eyes, how they would make the dream into a reality.

Emotion expanded in Ferro's chest and he embraced it, allowed himself to feel, wholly and completely, the love he had for the woman in front of him.

Then he pulled her into his arms. "I love it when you get excited about a project."

"I'm not boring you?"

"Never. You make me feel like life is one big adventure."

"Who me? I don't just look like a geek?"

He kissed her. "Julia Anderson, you look perfect to me."

"I may wear an elven robe to our product launch. Since I'm newly liberated and all."

"I'll still think you look perfect."

"Oh, really?"

"Yes," he said. "Because you're you. And you can never be anything less than perfect to me."

EPILOGUE

LAUNCHING AN ENTIRELY new line of cars was a pretty huge deal. And considering all the pretty huge deals Julia Anderson had experienced in her life, that was saying something. Computers, phones, tablets, true love…yeah, her life had been pretty full so far.

She looked out at the crowd, thousands of people filling the auditorium, and millions watching online, and took a deep breath, ready to get started unveiling the new line of Julerro automobiles. Julia had nearly gagged on that name, but when you said it fast, it really did work.

She sneaked a glance at her reflection in the monitors. Strange to be in color, bright pink in fact, for a presentation, but…she didn't need to avoid any colors anymore. She didn't need to try to blend in.

"Thank you for coming today to the product launch of what, I believe to be the biggest and best endeavor for both Datasphere and Anfalas."

The screen behind her flickered, and rather than the new logo for the company, Ferro's face appeared.

She turned and put her hands on her hips. "Um…excuse me, I seem to be getting interrupted. Mr. Calvaresi, you're aware that this is a product launch you have a stake in, aren't you?"

Ferro had elected to have her do the speaking for the

launch, since she was more experienced in "spectacle." She should have been suspicious at his willingness to share the spotlight.

Really, she should have been. She knew him well enough by now to know that she couldn't trust the man worth a darn. Except when it came to the important things like love, faithfulness and accepting her for who she was. On that score she could trust him perfectly.

"I am completely aware of that, Ms. Anderson. I'm not here to interrupt the launch. Much." He stood from wherever he was and disappeared from the screen, leaving only an empty chair and a black background.

"My partner," she said to the crowd, "seems to be acquiring some of my flair for the dramatic. Who knew he had it in him?"

Then she heard footsteps and looked to the left, to see Ferro walking out from behind the curtain. He was immaculate and perfect in a suit and tie—black, of course, her favorite color.

"I got an idea in my head last night and I just couldn't shake it," he said.

"It's too late to make any changes to the car."

The audience laughed and she was sure they thought it was scripted.

"That's not it. I have a question I need to ask and it can't wait, not for another moment."

"All right then, Calvaresi," she said, starting to tremble, "you better ask before the nice people get bored."

Ferro lowered himself to one knee in front of her, taking her hand in his. "Julia, I have spent my life alone. But this past year with you has erased all of it. I can't remember what it's like to be cold at night. All I know is what it feels like to go to sleep with your arms wrapped around me. I can't remember ever feeling detached, because with you, I feel everything. I want to be with you, always. You have blotted out my past, made me feel new. Clean. You have made my present happy, beautiful. Now I'm asking you to be my future, always. Julia will you marry me, and make me the happiest man alive?"

Julia sank down to her knees, too, not caring that there was a massive audience looking on. Nothing mattered but him, but this. "You know, you've pulled some pretty crazy stunts, but this…this wins."

"It only wins if you say yes." He reached into his pocket and pulled out a ring box. She couldn't even be bothered to look at the jewelry. She was too busy looking at his eyes, shining with so much emotion, so much love, it warmed her everywhere.

"Then yes. Yes, because…because where else am I going to find a man who will stay up all night with me and play video games? Where else am I going to find a man who loves me just like I am?"

He pulled her in close and kissed her. The entire auditorium filled with the roar of the crowd cheering them on.

"Any other reason?" he asked.

"Well, yes, the most compelling reason being that I want to spend the rest of my life with you."

"Money didn't bring me happiness. It didn't bring me peace. You did, Julia. And I can never thank you enough."

"I don't need you to thank me. Just love me. And kiss me."

And he did.

* * * * *

#3161 THE BILLIONAIRE'S TROPHY

A Bride for a Billionaire

Lynne Graham

When Bastian Christou sees his intern's photo on an escort website, he's shocked by both her double life *and* her stunning photo. With an ex-fiancée to keep at bay, Emmie Marshall might just be the best armor money can buy!

#3162 AN INHERITANCE OF SHAME

Sicily's Corretti Dynasty

Kate Hewitt

Angelo Corretti has one mistress—revenge. But once there was an innocent girl who gave him one spectacular night. Now, on the cusp of absolute power, Angelo will look into those eyes again and learn of the consequences he left behind.

#3163 PRINCE OF SECRETS

By His Royal Decree

Lucy Monroe

Prince Demyan Zaretsky does whatever it takes to protect his country. So seducing Chanel Tanner will be easy. And marriage? An unfortunate side effect. She unwittingly holds the economic stability of Volyarus in her hands...and he must secure it.

#3164 A ROYAL WITHOUT RULES

Royal & Ruthless

Caitlin Crews

Royal PA Adriana Righetti's latest assignment, keeping playboy Prince Patricio out of the headlines, is mission impossible. Particularly as Pato is intent on ruffling her seemingly uptight feathers! But is there more to this rebel royal than the world knows?

You can find more information on upcoming Harlequin® titles, free excerpts and more at www.Harlequin.com.

HPCNM0713RA

#3165 IMPRISONED BY A VOW
Annie West

Billionaire Joss Carmody knows the rules of this game—he'll shower his new wife with diamonds, and in return he'll use her land to expand his business. That's all he's ever wanted, but he hasn't banked on the attraction Leila awakens.

#3166 A DEAL WITH DI CAPUA
Cathy Williams

Behind Rosie Tom's beauty, Angelo Di Capua knows there is a deceitful gold digger. But his late wife has left Rosie a cottage on his country estate—and if she wants to stay, she'll have to make a deal with the devil!

#3167 DUTY AT WHAT COST?
Michelle Conder

To protect Princess Ava de Veers, bodyguard James Wolfe must keep his mind on the job. As the passion between them escalates, they find it harder and harder to resist. But as royalty, Ava knows that duty *always* comes at a cost....

#3168 THE RINGS THAT BIND
Michelle Smart

Nico Baranski is furious. Does his wife really think he'd just let her walk away? He'll use every sensual trick he knows to bring her back. And once he's got her where he wants her? He'll let her go. But only when *he's* ready!

You can find more information on upcoming Harlequin®
titles, free excerpts and more at www.Harlequin.com.

HPCNM0713RB